THE
ROMAN
QUESTS
THE ARCHERS OF ISCA

Also by Caroline Lawrence

THE ROMAN QUESTS
Escape from Rome

THE ROMAN MYSTERIES
I The Thieves of Ostia
II The Secrets of Vesuvius
III The Pirates of Pompeii
IV The Assassins of Rome
V The Dolphins of Laurentum
VI The Twelve Tasks of Flavia Gemina
VII The Enemies of Jupiter
VIII The Gladiators from Capua
IX The Colossus of Rhodes
X The Fugitive from Corinth
XI The Sirens of Surrentum
XII The Charioteer of Delphi
XIII The Slave-girl from Jerusalem
XIV The Beggar of Volubilis
XV The Scribes from Alexandria
XVI The Prophet from Ephesus
XVII The Man from Pomegranate Street

Trimalchio's Feast and Other Mini-mysteries
The Legionary from Londinium and Other Mini-mysteries

THE ROMAN MYSTERY SCROLLS
The Sewer Demon
The Poisoned Honey Cake
The Thunder Omen
The Two-faced God

THE P.K. PINKERTON MYSTERIES
The Case of the Deadly Desperados
The Case of the Good-looking Corpse
The Case of the Pistol-packing Widows
The Case of the Bogus Detective

THE ROMAN QUESTS

THE ARCHERS OF ISCA

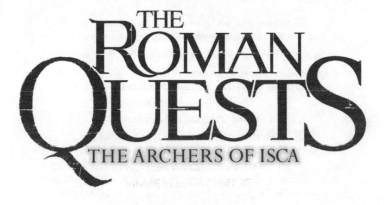

Caroline Lawrence

Orion
Children's Books

Orion Children's Books

First published in Great Britain in 2016 by Hodder and Stoughton
1 3 5 7 9 10 8 6 4 2

Text copyright © Roman Mysteries Ltd 2016
Map and illustrations copyright © Richard Russell Lawrence 2016

The moral rights of the author and illustrator have been asserted.

*All characters and events in this publication, other than those clearly
in the public domain, are fictitious and any resemblance to
real persons, living or dead, is purely coincidental.*

A CIP catalogue record for this book
is available from the British Library.

ISBN: 978 1 5101 0026 8

Typeset by Input Data Services Ltd, Bridgwater, Somerset

Printed and bound in Great Britain by Clays Ltd, St Ives plc

The paper and board used in this book are
made from wood from responsible sources.

Orion Children's Books
An imprint of
Hachette Children's Group
Part of Hodder and Stoughton
Carmelite House
50 Victoria Embankment
London EC4Y 0DZ

An Hachette UK Company

www.hachette.co.uk
www.hachettechildrens.co.uk

To the directors, staff and volunteers
at Butser Ancient Farm in Hampshire
for helping me imagine Iron Age Britain

BRITANNIA (ROMAN BRITAIN) IN AD 95

CALEDONIA

CARVETII

BRIGANTES

PARISI

DECEANGLI

CORNOVII

CORIELTAUVI

ICENI

ORDOVICI

DEMETAE

SILURES

DOBUNNI

GLEVUM

CATUVELLAUNI

TRINOVANTES

ISCA AUGUSTA

CORINIUM

AQUAE SULIS

SOFT HILL

ATREBATES

LONDINIUM

BELGAE

REGNI

CANTIACI

RUTUPIAE

DUMNONII

DUROTRIGES

FISHBOURNE

Salve (hello)!

Welcome to the second *Roman Quest*.

This story takes place in the ancient Roman province of Britannia in the year 95 AD, during the reign of the Emperor Domitian.

Some of the places in the story are sites that you can still visit today.

The main locations in this book are an Iron Age Village (like Butser Ancient Farm in Hampshire), *Aquae Sulis* (Bath Spa) and *Isca Augusta* (the fortress at Caerleon).

Most of the chapter headers are Latin, and refer to something in that chapter. See if you can guess what the words mean and then turn to the back of the book to see if you were right.

Vale (farewell)!

Caroline

I

Chapter One
DRUIDES

Fronto was eating flatbread with honey and staring into the flames of the central hearth fire when a shout of 'Kitten in the Deathwoods!' made him look up. Four lanky hunting dogs waiting in hopes of a scrap also looked up.

Three boys crowded through the single door of the roundhouse. They ran up to him.

'Kitten in the Deathwoods!' gasped the boy named Vindex. Like Fronto, he was fourteen years old. Unlike Fronto, he was a Briton, with pale skin, blond hair and smiling blue eyes.

Fronto squinted up at them. Were they joking? Sometimes it was hard to see people's expressions in the dimly lit roundhouse.

Vindex's older brother Bruvix kicked one of the dogs aside and spoke to Fronto slowly and loudly, as if speaking to a simpleton, 'Your sister's kitten went into the Deathwoods!'

Fronto was confused. Since the night they had fled Rome for Britannia, his sister and her kitten had been inseparable. It even rode on her shoulder. 'Isn't the kitten with Ursula?' he asked them.

'No,' said Vindex. 'She's gleaning in the barley field. Along with your brother Juba and your friend Bouda and all the other villagers.'

'We were on our way back here to get some more grain sacks,' said Bruvix, 'when Bellator saw the kitten go into the Deathwoods. You can save her if you hurry!'

But Fronto never did things in a hurry. He took another bite of bread and honey and chewed it thoughtfully. 'Why do you call it the "Deathwoods"?' he asked them.

'Because the spirits of our ancestors walk there,' said Bellator, the skinniest of the three.

'My grandfather saw a wolf there once,' added Vindex cheerfully.

'Also,' said Bruvix, 'some people say Druids lurk there, waiting to capture victims for their human sacrifices.'

Fronto swallowed hard and made the sign against evil. Even in Rome he had heard of those terrifying priests.

'I thought Paulinus killed all the Druids in this province a generation ago,' he said.

Bruvix shrugged. 'They say a few got away. And everyone knows the Druids reserve their most horrible torture methods for you Romans.'

Fronto tossed his last piece of bread and honey to one of the waiting dogs; he was not hungry any more.

'Why don't *you* look for the kitten?' he asked them.

'The woods are sacred to our ancestors,' said Bruvix. 'They are forbidden to us except on special days. But the elders wouldn't punish you for going there because you and your brother and sister and your friend Bouda are honoured guests.'

'Because you brought back our kidnapped brothers and sisters,' added Vindex.

'Go on, Fronto!' said Bellator. 'You're one of the Three Hooded Questers our bard has been singing about for the past two weeks. Go quest for the kitten.'

'We're supposed to be looking for lost children,' Fronto pointed out, 'not missing pets.'

'What's the matter?' said Bruvix. 'Are you afraid?'

Fronto looked up at Bruvix and the other two boys. He would be staying in this village for a few more weeks, maybe all winter, and he did not want to lose their respect.

He carefully brushed the crumbs from his dark brown cloak and stood up. 'All right,' he said. 'I'll look for the kitten in the Deathwoods. Do you have any weapons?'

'The Romans don't let us own weapons,' said Bruvix. 'Only hunting tools. Can you use a bow and arrows?'

Fronto nodded. 'Sometimes my father took me hunting when we went to our villa near Naples.'

'Then you can borrow mine.' Bruvix ran to a shadowy part of the roundhouse where bows and hunting javelins leaned against the white, inward-curving wall. He returned with a bow as tall as himself and a quiver of arrows.

'This is my best bow,' he said. 'And these are all my arrows. Make sure nothing happens to them.'

Fronto slung the quiver over his shoulder and took hold of the bow in his left hand. It was long and awkward, not like the small bow he had used in Italia. The dogs and boys followed him as he went to the door of the roundhouse and paused for a moment to tap three times on the doorframe at shoulder level: *right, left, right*. Then he stepped out, careful to use his right foot first.

As he emerged into the bright grey light of an overcast British morning he remembered what Julius Caesar had written about Druids: *They make huge statues out of wickerwork, which they fill with people and then set on fire, burning the victims as living sacrifices.*

As he moved down a path on a grassy slope between roundhouses and sheep pens, he remembered what a Greek historian had written: *Druids tell the future by stabbing their victims and then carefully noting how the blood flows, how the body twitches and what the guts look like.*

As he reached the stream by a grassy mound at the edge of the village, he remembered what Strabo had said: *Druids often shoot victims to death with so many arrows that they look like hedgehogs.*

Fronto gripped the tall bow more tightly with his left hand. With his right, he touched the small bronze statue of Jupiter that he always kept down the front of his tunic for protection.

The Deathwoods stood waiting for him just across the stream. On this side, friendly trees had dropped gold and orange leaves to carpet the ground. On the other side stood dark and ancient oaks. Their branches reached out to him like the twisted arms of burnt men. A few steps across a moss-covered log would take him over Cold Brook and into the brooding forest.

He looked at the boys.

'Here?' he said, pointing at the mossy log that bridged the brook. 'You saw the kitten crossing here?'

'Yes,' said skinny Bellator. 'I saw her go into the Deathwoods right there. She can't have gone far.' He looked as if he was trying not to smile.

Fronto hesitated. Something about this felt wrong.

'You're not scared, are you?' asked Bruvix.

Fronto stepped up onto the log and held the long bow horizontally so that it would help him balance. 'I'm not scared,' he told them. 'I'm excited.' It was something his father had taught him to say whenever he lacked courage. He repeated it, trying to say it with more confidence, 'I'm not scared; I'm excited!'

But as he took his first faltering steps across the log bridge, he muttered to himself, 'I'm not scared; I'm terrified!'

Chapter Two
LARVA

For as long as he could remember, Fronto had craved order and symmetry.

Growing up in a beautiful townhouse in Rome, his first memory had been helping sort his father's gems in order of size and colour. His second memory was of unrolling some of his father's scrolls. He'd hated not knowing what the black squiggles meant and had learned to read almost before he could walk.

By the age of five he knew the value of every Roman coin. A quick glance at the 'heads' side could tell him which emperor had issued it and a study of the 'ships' side could tell him in which month and year. By six he was reading Greek and by seven he had memorised the first four books of Virgil's epic poem, the *Aeneid*. By eight he knew all the *Aeneid* by heart and by nine he could recite half of Homer's *Iliad*, in Greek.

He could easily recite things he had learned by heart, but new ideas often made his thoughts freeze. It was the same in life. He hated anything unexpected or different. Most of all, he hated things beyond his control.

When he was five, his older brother Lucius had fallen sick with a fever. Fronto's parents had put Lucius on a couch in the winter triclinium, covered in furs and propped up with pillows.

This room had a view of the fruit garden in one of the villa's four inner courtyards. The doctor who had come to bleed Lucius daily told Fronto always to step over the threshold of a room with his right foot first. For extra good luck he could touch the doorway three times – *right, left, right* – as well.

But one time Fronto had forgotten.

He had run into his brother's sickroom to tell him something. He had been in such a hurry that he did not touch the doorframe three times or even step over with his right foot.

Lucius had died that afternoon, two days short of his seventh birthday.

That was when Fronto's obsession with leaving and entering different spaces had begun.

Now Fronto jumped down from the log bridge and looked around for a proper entrance to the Deathwoods so that he could cross the threshold properly.

He saw that two of the twisted, black-trunked trees seemed to form a kind of gateway, so he went to them. He reached out to touch them – *right, left, right* – and shuddered. The bark was damp to his touch, almost slimy. He stepped between the trees, being careful to lead with his right foot first. It was colder here, and damper. He put up the hood of his dark brown cloak.

'Meer?' he called. 'Where are you, Meer?'

Fronto felt foolish calling the name Meer. It was not even Latin. When he had first told Ursula this she only laughed. 'Meer doesn't speak Latin. She speaks Kitten and told me her name herself!'

'Meer?' he repeated. '*Hic, hic, hic!*'

He stopped and squatted down. Planting one end of the bow in the boggy ground, he used it to steady himself while he searched the forest floor for traces of the kitten's paw-prints. But all he saw were slimy leaves. Still, there was a sort of path. His knees cracked as he stood up again, and he reluctantly moved forward.

As he followed the slippery path deeper into the woods, he tried to muster his courage by thinking of all the frightening experiences he had survived over the past two months.

He had survived being robbed in Rome's graveyard during their midnight flight from the Emperor's henchmen. He still bore the tiny scar of a knife-prick on his neck.

He had survived a six-week sea voyage from Ostia to Britannia. It had ended with a storm so violent that the ship's goat had been washed overboard. At one point Fronto had been flying like a pennant from the yard arm – clinging by just one hand – when he heard the voice of some god in his head: *This is not your time.*

Here in Britannia he had survived another nighttime escape through marshes on the south coast as a tide came in. That was when they had saved a dozen blue-eyed, fair-haired children from being shipped to Rome as slaves.

Those children were all from this Belgae village, and that was why they were now honoured guests, welcome to stay as long as they liked. That was why the villagers brought him food and gifts all day. That was why he did not have to work in the fields if he preferred to eat bread and honey by the fire. That was why he could venture into these terrifying sacred woods without rebuke: because he and his siblings had saved the children.

He and his siblings, and the girl named Bouda.

Just the thought of her copper-coloured hair and leaf-green eyes made Fronto feel a little braver.

He stopped. While he had been thinking about Bouda, the path had disappeared and he was now knee-deep in bracken.

Not the tender green ferns of spring, but the dying ferns of autumn: yellow, brown, even black. They stank of rot and decay.

He had forgotten his mission: to look for the kitten. Meer was tiny and could not have got this far. He wondered that she could even have crossed the mossy log bridge. Bellator must have been mistaken.

As he turned to go back, his stomach twisted. The woods looked different facing this way. Darker. Thicker. Closer. As if the trees had all taken a step towards him while his back was turned.

'Meer?' he said. His voice caught halfway down his throat and sounded like a stranger's. 'Meer? Where are you?'

There was no reply. Just the wind moaning in the branches.

'I'm not scared,' he told himself. 'I'm excited. Jupiter Ammon,' he whispered, 'give me courage.'

As he started back, he felt the little hairs on the back of his neck rise up. Someone was watching him.

Someone or *something*!

He stopped and pushed back the hood of his cloak so that he could see to the sides as well as straight ahead. The soft fall of the woollen hood made the arrows rattle in the quiver on his back. He reached over his shoulder and plucked one out. He noticed the arrowhead was flint, but it seemed as sharp as iron so he notched it into the deer-sinew string of the bow.

That made him feel a little safer.

Until he felt the prickle again.

'There's nothing here,' he told himself as he slowly scanned the forest around him. 'No birds, no squirrels, no insects. Nothing to hurt me. I'm not scared; I'm excited.'

Then he saw it.

Staring at him from parted brambles perhaps twenty paces

away was a terrifying face. The man's hair was set in stiff white spikes and his beard took the form of three dangling blue snakes. More terrifying than spiky hair and snaky beard were his glaring black eyes.

With a yelp of terror Fronto dropped the bow and arrow.

Then he ran.

Chapter Three
VICUS

U rsula loved living in the village at the foot of the hill.

From a distance, the seven roundhouses reminded her of pointy mushrooms. Smoke from central hearth fires seeped through the conical thatched roofs. Five of the roundhouses contained a different extended family. Of the remaining two, one was the Women's House and one was the Men's House. There were also much smaller mushrooms: the grain stores, the chicken coop and stables. There were even beehives with their own little conical roofs.

The village nestled between two woods with a hill at its back and a brook on one side. Before lay a patchwork of barley fields and grazing land. It was called Soft Hill after the sheep-dotted green hill that stood as a windbreak and seemed to watch over the settlement.

When she and her brothers and the British girl Bouda had first arrived, driving their ox-drawn carruca down a path between fields into the village at dusk, the parents of the kidnapped children had run out to meet them. They had cried and laughed and hugged their children, just as any Roman parent would have done.

As the children's rescuers, she and her brothers and Bouda

had been welcomed into the biggest roundhouse. It belonged to Velvinnus, the chieftain of the village.

In her family villa back in Rome, Ursula had slept alone in a small, square cubicle.

Here, everyone slept together in one big space. If a baby woke up crying in the night and the mother was too tired to sing it to sleep, one of its aunts or older sisters would take it.

At home in Rome, her mother had refused to have pets, apart from Ursula's talking bird.

Here, the big hunting dogs wandered in and out as they liked. Some people even used them as pillows.

In Rome, her mother sang songs at the loom.

Here a man called Bardus sang of their exploits every evening. He sang about the Three Hooded Questers who had travelled across the nameless ocean to Britannia. As he strummed his harp, the bard told how they had travelled by mule-cart and on foot from Londinium to the south coast just in time to save the village children from being shipped to faraway Rome.

He even sang of her: telling how the youngest Quester carried a kitten on one shoulder and a talking bird on the other.

Now, well into their third week in the village, Ursula had gone with Bouda and her brother and almost all the other villagers to glean the last of the barley before the winter frost came. She and some of the younger children were returning with small sacks of barley when they heard laughter from the direction of the Cold Brook.

Some of the little children put down their sacks and ran, so Ursula did, too.

'*Meeer!*' protested her kitten Meer, clinging tightly to her left shoulder.

'*Oh Pollux!*' said her talking bird, Loquax, and he fluttered up from her right shoulder. He had been gleaning barley, too, but had not saved any in a sack.

As they reached the brook, Ursula saw some boys standing with their backs to her.

'What is it?' she asked them in Brittonic. 'What's happened?'

'The oldest Roman boy,' laughed Bellator, without looking round. 'He's fallen in the brook!'

'We tricked him into going into the Deathwoods!' said Bruvix. 'We told him his sister's kitten was—' He had been turning to look at them but stopped when he saw Ursula. She saw his eyes go to Meer on her shoulder.

'Oh, there it is!' he said in an unnaturally loud voice. 'Look, Fronto! Your sister's kitten was with her after all. Bellator must have made a mistake.'

Two of the boys laughed again.

Angrily pushing through them, Ursula saw her elder brother standing knee deep in the brook. His curly black hair was dripping wet and his long brown cloak was sodden. Beside him, the mossy log was askew. He must have fallen off it.

Fronto's eyes were wide and she could see his chest rising and falling as he gasped for breath. He did not look angry; he looked frightened.

'Druid!' he cried. 'I saw a Druid in the Deathwoods!'

'You saw what?' Bruvix sounded more scornful than alarmed.

'A Druid!' gasped Fronto again. 'I saw a Druid in the Deathwoods!'

'*Druid in the Deathwoods!*' repeated Loquax, fluttering back down onto Ursula's shoulder. '*Druid in the Deathwoods!*'

At this, the British boys laughed again. Some of them began to chant: 'Druid in the Deathwoods!'

15

'There are no more Druids!' cried Bruvix. 'We made it up!' He laughed even harder and slapped his own leg.

'Then it must have been a ghost!' Fronto cried. 'I saw a man with spiky hair and snakes for a beard . . .' he trailed off and Ursula saw his dark skin flush even darker. His shoulders slumped as he realised they were mocking him. Although she was five years younger than Fronto, she felt fiercely protective of him.

'Fronto,' she said, stepping forward. 'Come out of the stream or you'll catch a fever.'

She went to the bank of the stream and held out her hand. One of the British boys joined her there and also held out his hand to Fronto. 'Bruvix is always doing this,' Vindex muttered under his breath. 'He even had me fooled.'

Fronto waded towards them and stretched out his dripping hands.

Together, Ursula and Vindex pulled him out of the water.

'Come back to the roundhouse, Fronto,' said Ursula. 'We'll sit you by the hearth fire and get you dry clothes.'

'Not so fast.' Bruvix stood blocking their way. 'Where's my bow? And my arrows?'

Fronto hung his head. 'I dropped the bow in the Deathwoods. And most of the arrows are in the water.'

Bruvix stepped forward. 'Then you'd better fish them out!' he cried, and pushed Fronto back into the water.

Everyone except Bouda, Ursula and Vindex burst into laughter, with Bruvix laughing hardest of all.

Ursula gasped with outrage. 'You big bully!' she cried, and gave Bruvix an almighty shove that sent him into the brook as well.

Chapter Four
FOCUS

Fronto had put on dry tunics and felt slippers and was towelling his hair by the central hearth fire back in the chieftain's roundhouse when Vindex ran up to him.

'Dallara wants to see you!'

'Dallara, the wise woman of the village?' asked Ursula. She was sitting beside her brother gently drying Meer, who had been drenched by Bruvix's big splash.

Vindex nodded. His face was serious but his eyes were smiling.

Fronto put down the linen towel and said, 'You're one of the boys who tricked me.'

'I didn't know it was a trick!' said Vindex. 'Bruvix and Bellator had the rest of us fooled, too.'

'Then why are your eyes smiling?'

Vindex shrugged. 'That's just the way they are!'

'He's telling the truth,' said Ursula. 'He was the only one who didn't laugh when Bruvix pushed you in the water.'

Vindex lowered his voice. 'Bruvix hates you because he and Bellator were supposed to be guarding the children when they were kidnapped. And because you sit around eating bread and honey while the rest of us have to work.'

'But your grandfather said I could stay here if I wanted,' protested Fronto.

'I know,' said Vindex. 'Come on. I'll show you the way to Dallara.' He pulled Fronto to his feet and then he held out his hand to Ursula.

'She wants to see me, too?' asked Ursula in surprise.

'Yes,' said Vindex. 'Your brother and Bouda are already with her.'

Fronto and Ursula exchanged a glance. They had been in the village two and a half weeks and had not yet seen the mysterious wise woman who lived in the strangely decorated women's roundhouse.

'Is she going to ask us to leave?' Fronto said. He knew that even the chieftain of the village obeyed Dallara.

'I don't think so,' said Vindex. As he led the way out of the roundhouse, he turned his head. 'Did you really see someone in the Deathwoods?' he asked Fronto over his shoulder.

'Yes,' said Fronto, touching the door of the roundhouse before stepping outside.

'Was it like a giant man made of woven hazel branches?'

'No,' said Fronto. 'It was a real man with spiky white hair and . . .' he trailed off. Had he really seen blue snakes where a beard should be?

Outside, it had started to rain, but the overhang of the thatched roof gave some shelter as he and Ursula followed Vindex round the curve of the wall. About a third of the way round it they made a dash across wet green grass to a smaller roundhouse. This one had black swirls painted on the pale outer wall, as if some kind of magic vine had once curled round it and then died, leaving only its shadow.

The skull of a four-horned ram glared down at them from

above the doorway. Fronto made the sign against evil and was careful to touch the doorframe *right, left, right* as he entered.

A hearth fire in the centre of this smaller roundhouse showed some women by the wall on his left, grinding something pungent in a mortar. Against the right-hand wall he glimpsed a girl sleeping in furs. And propped up against the opposite wall straight ahead was an ancient woman. She raised a claw-like hand and beckoned them over.

As he got closer Fronto saw that she was covered with a chequered rug of blue, yellow and green, the colours of the Belgae. Beside her sat his brother Juba and pretty Bouda. Juba stood up. He had the same black hair, brown skin and grey-green eyes as Fronto, but he was skinnier and younger.

Bouda regarded Fronto with her cat-like green eyes. He remembered the look of scorn on her face when he had been in the brook shouting about the Druid in the woods. His face grew hot.

'Fronto. Ursula. Come and sit on this side of me,' the old woman said in Brittonic. She patted some sheepskins on her right. 'Vindex? You stay too. I dreamt of five.'

The three of them sat on the old lady's right with Fronto closest to her head. Close up, he could see a strange grey film covered the old woman's blue eyes. Her gaze was fixed and he realised she was blind.

'Put that beaver-skin cloak around you, Fronto.' The old woman's voice was croaky but strong. 'I can hear your teeth chattering.'

Fronto found the folded beaver-skin cloak and pulled it around his shoulders. It was the softest fur he had ever touched, and deliciously warm.

'I have just been speaking to your brother Juba,' said the old

19

woman. 'The bard has been singing me your story: how you came from the land of the Romans to our village. Then last night I dreamt of five strangers. Were there five?' She groped for Bouda's hand and held it up. 'I only know of this one, and the three of you. But who is the fifth?'

Fronto looked at his brother and sister. What was the old lady talking about?

'Maybe you mean Castor,' said Ursula. 'He's a rich Roman boy a little older than Juba. He owned the ship that brought us here to Britannia.'

Bouda added, 'He's looking for his brother who was kidnapped as a baby.'

'Perhaps he is the fifth,' said the old woman. 'If so, your paths will cross again.' She cocked her head in Ursula's direction. 'Are you the girl who walks with a kitten on one shoulder and a talking raven on the other?'

'He's not a raven,' said Ursula politely. 'But he speaks. Don't you, Loquax?'

'*Ave, Domitian!*' said Loquax.

'May I hold your kitten?'

The old lady cupped her gnarled hands and Ursula placed Meer in them.

'*Meeer!*' said Meer.

Old Dallara stroked the kitten. 'Ursula, you have the gift of fur and feathers.'

Ursula frowned at Dallara and opened her mouth, but before she could speak, the old lady said, 'Fronto, are you the boy who went into the Deathwoods?'

'Yes. Some boys told me my sister's kitten had gone there. They lied.'

'How do the three of you come to speak our language?'

20

'Castor – the boy who owned the ship we came on – made us speak only Brittonic on the voyage here. The crew were from Britannia,' he added.

The old lady gave Meer back to Ursula and took Fronto's hand in both of hers. The skin over the bones of her hands was soft and cool, and mottled with pale brown spots.

'Ah!' she said. 'Sailors' calluses on a soft hand. And I can tell you are a watery one. You need the refining fire of discipline.'

'Yes,' Fronto sighed. 'My father always told me I was . . .' He hesitated and then said in Latin, 'phlegmatic.'

'I do not know that word.'

'It means my element is water. It means I am easy-going and sometimes lazy. A good follower but rarely a leader.'

'And yet you are the eldest?'

Fronto glanced at his brother who sat cross-legged on the other side of the woman. '*Now* I am the eldest,' he said. 'Once we had an older brother, but he died of fever when I was five.'

'Ah! That explains why you do not have the spirit of the eldest. Tell me again what brought you here? Your brother's account only took me as far as the seaport called Ostia.'

In halting Brittonic, Fronto told her how they had spent six weeks on a merchant ship sailing from Ostia to Britannia in order to escape soldiers sent by the Emperor Domitian.

'Are you telling me the most powerful man in the known world is your enemy?'

'Yes,' Fronto admitted. 'Domitian is our enemy.'

'*Ave, Domitian!*' added Loquax.

'You are rich?'

Fronto glanced at his brother, who gave him a small nod.

'We *were* rich,' he said. 'But now we have nothing. Only our household gods and the clothes on our backs.'

'And yet you turned down the chance to live with a wealthy relative. Instead, you rescued twelve of our children, abducted and sold into slavery by black-hearted Durotrigan raiders.'

'Yes,' said Fronto. 'My brother and sister here made the decision.'

'You did not support their decision?'

'Of course I supported them. Juba always does what is right, and my sister is the bravest person I know.'

'You are brave, too, I think.' The old woman patted his hand and then released it.

Fronto remembered how he had run out of the woods and fallen into the stream. He remembered the boys' laughter. And the look of scorn on Bouda's pretty face. He could not even meet her eyes now.

He hung his head. 'Not really,' he mumbled.

'You went into the Deathwoods to save your sister's kitten.'

'Her kitten was never in the Deathwoods. It was with her all the time. She was gleaning barley with the other villagers.'

'But you didn't know that. You were afraid and went into the woods all the same.'

'I suppose. But when I saw the Druid I was terrified. I dropped Bruvix's bow and arrows.'

The old lady nodded. 'I sent him back to get them. And I have a bow and arrows for you to keep. Vindex? Fetch the bow by the wall.'

Vindex got up, went to the wall and brought back a beautiful bow made of ash and willow. Unlike Bruvix's tall bow, this one was small and strongly curved.

'That is a priceless composite bow from Scythia,' said the old woman. 'And my own hand-made arrows. I want you to have them.'

'Really?' Fronto's eyes opened wide.

'Really. Now tell me more about your Druid.'

Fronto sighed. 'It probably wasn't a Druid. It was probably one of the boys with lime in his hair and a blue woollen beard.'

'I am old enough to remember Druids,' said the old lady. 'Describe the face.'

Fronto described the frightening face with its staring black eyes, spiky white hair and beard of three dangling blue snakes.

The old woman sat very still for several long moments. Then she murmured something in Britonnic. 'It is time.'

'What?' said Fronto. 'What did you say?'

She shook her head. 'Nothing,' she said. 'Tell me Fronto. Have you and the others been to the sacred springs of Aquae Sulis?'

Fronto felt a pang of guilt. 'Not yet,' he said. 'But three weeks ago, we vowed to dedicate an altar to the gods if they brought us safely here.'

Dallara nodded. 'Then you must fulfil the vow. The sanctuary is only two hours' walk from here,' she said. 'I believe the four of you should go there without delay. Vindex?' she said.

The British boy looked up at her, his blue eyes wide. 'Yes?'

She was frowning. 'I dreamt of five, so you must go with them to be their guide.'

Vindex looked worried. 'Shall I ask some of the older boys to go with us? In case of Durotrigan raiders?'

'Did they protect the little ones who were kidnapped?'

'No,' admitted Vindex. 'But Father won't be happy about us going alone.'

'Your father will submit to my wishes. And I dreamt of five. The five of you must go to fulfil your vow and seek your destinies at once.'

'Now?' said Juba. 'Do you want us to go right now?'

'Yes. You must never delay thanking the gods or fulfilling a vow.'

For once Fronto was the first to act. 'Dallara is right,' he said. 'We can't afford to displease the gods!' He shrugged off the beaver-skin cloak, grasped his new bow and rose to his feet. 'We'd better go now!'

Chapter Five
GEMMAE

The sun broke through the clouds as the five of them came out of the woods and onto the Roman road that would take them to the sanctuary of Aquae Sulis with its magic hot spring.

Juba was glad that they were finally going. Dedicating an altar would mark the end of their quest. They had returned the kidnapped children to their village and in so doing had hopefully found a place where the Emperor's men would not find them.

Walking always lifted his spirits and for a moment his hopes soared: They had done it! They had survived!

But what would they do now?

What would their lives be without parents or older relatives to help them?

He liked the village, and the villagers, but it was a strange life. It was not Roman. His father had hoped that Juba would learn rhetoric and practise law. What would his father say if he knew Juba had been gleaning barley like a common farm slave?

And what of Ursula and Fronto? Until now their lives had progressed smoothly, with Fronto heading for the army, Ursula to marriage, and himself to the law. But the death of his parents and their flight from Rome had put an end to all their goals.

A moment before he had felt as light as a skylark.

Now he felt as burdened as Hercules after he took the world on his shoulders.

'Did you hear what I said?' asked Bouda, tugging his cloak. 'Are you even listening?'

'I'm sorry.' Juba turned his head to look at her. 'What did you say?'

'I just wanted to know how you plan to pay for an altar,' she said. 'Will you sell your Minerva gem?'

Juba touched the priceless gem on a chain around his neck. It was a sardonyx in shades of brown and white – carved to show the goddess Minerva in profile.

He shook his head. 'I'd hate to sell this. My mother gave it to me. It's the only thing of hers I have left.'

For a moment he considered telling her what he had not told anyone: that there was a fortune in gems sewn into the seams of his grubby cloak. Bouda and his brother and sister knew the Pearl of Iris had been hidden in his cloak, but he had not told them that it was only one of many jewels.

The thought of the fortune those gems could bring lifted the burden of worry from his mind, and his pace quickened. He could buy or even build a villa here in this remote edge of the Empire. He could live quietly with his brother and sister under a new name. They never need worry again.

Bouda was running to keep up with him and tugging his cloak again. 'So where will you get the money to buy an altar?' she demanded. 'And why are you smiling?'

Juba thought quickly. 'I sold our two oxen and the carruca to Velvinnus,' he lied. 'He gave me three gold coins. That should be enough to buy a small altar.'

He felt her gaze and kept his eyes straight ahead and his expression serious.

'It's too bad you don't have any more pearls sewn into the seams of your cloak,' she said pointedly.

Juba managed not to gape at her. Had she guessed his secret? He kept his jaw firmly clenched and offered up a silent prayer of thanks when Vindex said, 'What's a "pearl"? I don't know that word.'

Bouda said the word in Brittonic but Vindex shrugged. 'I still don't know what that is. Unlike you, I haven't seen much of the world. I've only been as far as Aquae Sulis and once to the big fortress at Isca. Isca Augusta,' he added. 'Not Isca Dumnoniorum.'

The road was empty at this point and as Ursula joined them, they were walking five abreast.

'A pearl is a kind of gemstone that grows in the sea,' she explained. 'They're perfectly round and white but if you look closely you can see colours in them.' She turned to Juba. 'Are you sure you don't have any more?' she asked. She reached out to grasp his cloak. 'Maybe they're hidden in the seams here.'

'Get off!' Juba cried, jumping back. And when they all stared at him he said, 'I have to relieve myself. I'm just going behind those trees. Keep walking. I'll catch you up.'

'You just went,' said Fronto.

Juba glared at him. 'I have to go again!'

He jumped over the roadside ditch and went behind a tree and turned his back to them in case they were watching. But instead of peeing, he took the ivory handled dagger from its sheath on his belt and then fingered the front edge of his cloak beneath the boxwood toggle.

Without knowing it, Bouda had been right: his mother had sewn two dozen gems into the seam, twelve either side. She had done it in such a way that he only had to cut one stitch to release a new gem. He felt for a medium-sized bump – one the size of a pea rather than a chickpea – cut the stitch and pushed out the gem.

He cursed as it fell onto the ground, and quickly bent to pick it up. It was a pale orange carnelian, flat and oval, with Pegasus the flying horse carved into it. He cursed again. It was valuable, but might not raise enough to buy an altar.

Cutting a stitch on the other side of the cloak flap, he released a black pearl. Now *that* was worth something.

He sheathed his knife and stood silent for a moment.

Why hadn't he told the others?

Bouda was the answer. In Londinium she had belonged to a gang of cutpurses. He knew she would do almost anything for riches.

He put the two gems in the coin part of his belt and caught up with them at the crest of a hill. They were standing four abreast, breathing hard and looking down into the valley.

'Look, Juba!' gasped Ursula. 'That's the sanctuary with the magic hot water!'

She was pointing down at a cluster of Roman-looking buildings surrounded by the silver loop of a river.

'Is that it?' Juba asked Vindex. 'Is that Aquae Sulis?'

'Yes!' Vindex replied. 'See the building with the roofs curved like barrels and the dome and the steam rising up? That's the new bath-house. And the tallest building with the pitched roof and four columns is the temple of Sulis Minerva.'

'Look at all the altars in the courtyard behind the temple,' said Ursula.

Juba nodded. 'With that many altars,' he said, 'there's sure to be a place to buy one down there.'

Ursula pointed again. 'Those coloured awnings on either side of the road must be market stalls.'

Vindex nodded. 'They belong to bankers, money-changers and sellers of votive objects, souvenirs and hot food.'

'Hot food?' said Fronto. 'Can we get something to eat? I'm starving.'

'And can we bathe in the magic hot waters, too?' asked Ursula.

'Of course,' said Juba. 'You can eat and bathe while I find a stonemason or someone who sells altars.'

And, as they started down the hill, he touched the figurine of a god that he carried down the front of his tunic and offered a silent prayer: *Please, Mercury, god of travellers, merchants and money. Guide me to an honest banker and may I get a good price for the Pegasus carnelian and the Black Pearl.*

Chapter Six
AQUAE SULIS

They were halfway down the hill when a light shower of rain made Fronto, Juba and Ursula put up their hoods. Vindex was wearing a blue felt skullcap embroidered with yellow. Bouda's fur-trimmed blue cape did not have a hood, so she covered her head with a leaf-green palla that matched her eyes and made her coppery hair look almost orange. Fronto tried not to stare. Instead, he concentrated on muttering *right, left, right*, for drizzle was unlucky.

From behind them the rumble of wheels and clank of a bell warned them of an overtaking ox-cart.

'We'd better walk single file,' said Juba, and led them onto the beaten path beside the slick Roman road.

Fronto didn't mind Juba taking the lead. He was more concerned with what might come out of the woods on either side. Vindex had told them to watch out for Durotrigan raiders, for this was the same stretch of road on which the children had been seized a month before.

He relaxed a little when a road from the south joined theirs and they became part of a throng. He saw two strong men carrying an old man on a stretcher and a canvas-covered mule-cart full of British women.

A quick-striding man with a wide-brimmed straw hat and a walking stick overtook them, and they overtook a Roman woman and her slave girl. The Roman woman had a tall wig of curly black hair and the girl held a pink linen parasol to protect her mistress from the rain. The woman's withered left hand was twisted behind her in a strange position. Also on the path were several couples and a family with three young children.

As they reached the bottom of the hill, Fronto saw the stalls lining the road and his stomach growled as he caught the scent. 'Look!' he said. 'That one is selling hot sausages!'

'Why don't you all go and get one?' said Juba. 'I'll meet you there in a few moments. I just want to change one of my gold coins for coppers at that banker's stall. Buy me a sausage?' he called over his shoulder.

'You don't have to change your money,' said Vindex. 'My father gave me some coppers so that we could all visit the baths.'

But Juba was already standing before a table laden with coins, weights and a balance. A man in a toga stood behind it and a fierce-looking dog crouched like a panting Sphinx underneath.

Fronto turned back to the sausage stall. He was hungry but he also liked to take his time when choosing so he waited to see what the others would have. Bouda chose wild boar sausages with pepper, Vindex went for black sausage made with blood and Ursula – who ate no meat – opted for soft green herby cheese called moretum on celery sticks.

Fronto finally chose a steaming wild boar sausage without pepper. It was presented to him wrapped in a cool leaf of pale green cabbage. Once it had cooled off, he devoured it and the cabbage wrapper, too. 'I'll have another,' he said to the sausage-seller.

'Look, Fronto!' cried Ursula from the stall next door.

When he came over with his second sausage she pointed at square sheets of dark grey lead, small and thin. Some had writing on them and some were blank.

'What are these for?' Fronto asked the old man behind the stall.

'The goddess in the Sacred Spring hears every prayer and every curse,' said the man, whose face looked like a dried apple. 'Some people throw in coins, asking her to grant their dearest wish. But if you have an enemy or someone you wish was dead, you write a curse on one of these sheets, roll it up and toss it in the spring. They never fail,' he added.

Juba came up to them, and Fronto noticed he was wearing a rare smile.

'Juba,' cried Ursula. 'Look at these curse tablets. Shall we curse the Emp—?'

'Shhh!' Juba grabbed her arm and tugged her away from the stalls and onto a bridge. 'Don't even think of mentioning him,' he hissed, and then turned to Fronto. 'Did you get me a sausage?'

Fronto had been waiting for his second wild boar sausage to cool, but he nobly held it out. 'Here.'

'Thanks.' Juba took a bite. 'Have any of you seen a mason?'

'You can usually hear them before you see them,' said Vindex.

As the five of them stopped to listen for the distinctive sound of chisel on stone, Fronto noticed people looking back at them and whispering. A few were even pointing.

'What is it?' hissed Bouda behind him. 'Why are they pointing at you?'

Vindex cupped his ear and then laughed. 'They're calling you the Three Hooded Questers! Our bard has made you famous!' His voice made more heads turn, and the muttering grew more excited.

Fronto and the others were still on the bridge when a dark-haired woman darted forward and threw herself on the street in front of Juba.

'Bring my son back!' she cried. 'Bring my son back to me.'

Judging from her brown hair and dark eyes, Fronto guessed that she was not of the Belgae tribe like Vindex. Also, the stripes on her long tunic were orange and brown.

Behind him he heard Vindex hiss, 'A Durotrigan! They're our enemies.'

As the woman reached out to touch the hem of Juba's cloak, Fronto saw his brother's eyes open wide in alarm. Juba clutched his cloak tighter, as if he were afraid she might steal it.

But the woman had already moved over to touch Ursula's cloak and now she was tugging *his*! Fronto stared at her in astonishment. What was she doing? Was she mad? As she nodded her thanks and backed away, a blond man and woman also fell to their knees. They wore tunics of tan and pine-green. 'Our daughter went missing last month,' said the man, lifting eyes full of pain first to Fronto and then the other two. 'Her name is Dirtha, from Calleva Atrebatum.'

The woman whispered, 'We think she was abducted by *Druids*. She said she had been speaking to one. The next week she was gone.'

This couple also touched the hems of their three cloaks and then quickly retreated.

'My son is gone, too!' said a man with dark, curly hair and pale eyes. 'His name is Dubonus. We live across the water to the west, by the big fortress.'

Fronto glanced at Vindex in puzzlement.

'What's happening?' Juba voiced Fronto's question.

Vindex shrugged. 'They must have heard how you rescued the children from our village,' he said. 'During the day our bard visits bards in other villages to exchange stories and news. Your story is obviously the most popular at the moment.'

'We came here to ask the goddess to bring back our children,' said the next woman, looking from one to the other of them. 'Then we saw you. Our daughter's name is Bircha. Tonight would have been her fourteenth Samhain. Our son Bolianus went missing at the same time, a week ago. He is a year older.'

Fronto didn't know the word *Samhain* but he understood the girl was fourteen and her older brother fifteen.

'Aren't they old enough to leave home if they want?' Fronto frowned.

'We need them in the field and at the loom,' said the father.

Fronto spread his hands, palms up, in a gesture of defeat. 'I don't know what we can do,' he said.

'All we ask,' said the parents, 'is that if you see them you will tell us or send word!'

Juba stepped forward. 'Dirtha, Dubonus, Bircha and Bolianus,' he said in a clear voice. 'If we come across any of them – or any other lost children – we will post a notice here at this sanctuary. Now please let us go. We must fulfil a vow.'

But the next woman to throw herself at Fronto's feet was the Roman woman with the withered hand.

'Heal my hand, O Hooded Ones!' she cried.

Like the others, she touched the hems of their cloaks with her good hand. Her slave girl reached forward, too, almost

34

poking Fronto in the eye with one of the ivory-tipped spokes of her pink parasol.

Fronto looked at Vindex.

'They think you're some kind of gods!' Vindex explained.

Now more people were pushing forward, reaching out their hands, hoping for just a touch of Juba's tawny cloak, Ursula's pine-green or Fronto's dark brown one.

'Oh!' Ursula squealed, staggering back.

Fronto's heart was pounding, but his thoughts were suddenly frozen.

Thankfully, Juba had the sense to cry in his orator's voice. 'We can try to find your loved ones, but we aren't gods. We can't heal. We may have darker skin than you, but we are human like you!'

At this, the crowd fell back a little and their excited murmur died down.

But a moment later the clouds parted to let a slanting beam of sunshine fall upon the three of them.

'Look!' cried a woman in Brittonic. 'The sun god Belenus is pointing them out with his beam.'

'And there's a rainbow behind them!' called another woman.

'It's a sign,' squealed a third.

'They *are* the Three Hooded Spirits!' cried a man in Latin.

Everyone cheered and the people pushed forward again, shoving Vindex and Bouda out of the way.

The low stone wall of the bridge was behind them and Fronto felt its top edge digging hard into the small of his back. Beside him Ursula squealed again and he could hear Juba grunting.

Fronto closed his eyes and prayed, 'Please, Jupiter Ammon. Save us!'

But as he felt himself being pushed further and further back, he knew this was the end. The three of them must either be crushed against the wall of the bridge, or fall into the water to smash their heads on the rocks below.

Chapter Seven
LORICA SQUAMATA

Just when Fronto was about to give up on fighting off the crowd and let himself be pushed over the bridge into the rocky river below, rescue came from an unexpected place.

The brassy blare of a trumpet froze the reaching hands.

The distinctive stomp of hobnail boots made people shrink back.

The deep-voiced chant of a marching song made the crowd scatter. Roman soldiers were coming, and nobody could stand in their way.

Fronto saw Ursula huddled by his feet at the base of the low wall. He put his arm around her. With Juba's help he got her off the bridge and onto the grassy verge of the road. She collapsed on the grass by one of the stalls and he sat beside her, muttering *right, left, right.*

'Are you all right?' Juba asked her.

Ursula nodded. 'They almost crushed me. I'm so glad I left Meer and Loquax in the village. They would have been terrified.'

'Are any of you hurt?' cried Vindex, running up with Bouda.

They all shook their heads. Fronto saw that the British boy looked genuinely concerned. For once his eyes were not smiling.

But Bouda seemed angry. 'It's not easy being famous, is it?' she snapped.

'It wasn't our fault the crowds took us for gods,' replied Juba hotly.

'We were almost crushed to death!' cried Ursula.

'So were we!' said Bouda.

Fronto noticed that her skin was paler than usual and her lips had no colour. *She's afraid!* he thought. *I freeze when I'm afraid, but she lashes out.*

'We're sorry, Bouda,' he said, standing up. 'We didn't mean to get separated from you.' He put his hand on her shoulder and felt her trembling under the blue cape. 'Are you all right?'

She looked at him and he saw the anger fade. Suddenly she looked very young and vulnerable. He remembered she was only eleven years old. Not much older than Ursula.

'We're sorry,' he said again, but his words were drowned out by another blare of brass and the deafening stomp of the soldiers who had now reached the bridge.

Fronto and the others turned to look at their rescuers. Leading the column were three white horses, followed by five ranks of four horses each, and behind them ten ranks of eight soldiers marching abreast. The rider in the middle carried a banner showing a red scorpion on yellow. On either side of him rode officers: a centurion and an optio.

'They're not legionaries!' he cried. 'They're auxiliaries! Syrian archers, probably.'

The soldiers were chanting a marching song:

For seventeen days we've been on the road,
We've sweat in our helmets and lice in our clothes!

So clear out the people and bring on the steam,
The Syrian Scorpions need to get clean!

Fronto felt a grin spread across his face. The soldiers had saved them! Just being near them made him feel braver.

'Is it the same unit we saw on the road to Fishbrook earlier this month?' Juba said in Fronto's ear.

'I don't think so,' Fronto replied. 'They didn't have horses. This must be a century of part-mounted auxiliaries.'

'These ones are much more splendid than the ones we saw before!' said Bouda. 'Some of them have armour like fish scales!'

Fronto nodded. 'That type of armour is called *lorica squamata*!' He had to raise his voice to be heard above the tramp of their hobnailed boots. 'Arrows just bounce off. And their pointy helmets are based on ancient Assyrian models.'

'Why are their tunics so long?' shouted Ursula.

'They need long tunics for the hot and dusty land they come from.'

'I think they're wonderful!' cried Bouda.

'You do?' Fronto glanced down at her, to see if she was making fun of him.

'Yes,' said Bouda. The colour had returned to her cheeks. 'I love how their armour and helmets flash in the sun.'

Now the archers were singing a new chant:

Bring out your women and bring out your beer
The Syrian Scorpions soon will be here!

'We'd better plan what we can do after they've gone past,' said Juba, 'or we'll be mobbed again.'

'Let's go into the baths after them,' suggested Fronto.

'Good idea!' cried Vindex. 'Your skin is almost the same as the Syrians'. You can stay close to them and nobody will know. You could even pass for a soldier.'

'You think so?' said Fronto. His heart was thumping.

'Of course! You're tall enough. Go sneak in after them!'

Fronto turned to go and then turned back. 'Come with me,' he said to Vindex. 'Not all of them were dark skinned. Two of them looked Italian and one had fair skin like yours.'

'All right!' Vindex's blue eyes sparkled. 'Will you come, too, Juba?'

Juba shook his head. 'You two might pass for recruits but I'm too short and skinny. I'll stay out here and order an altar. But you go ahead; it's a good idea for us to split up. Also, you should try the magic waters here.'

'What about us?' Ursula said. 'What will we do?'

Juba looked at Vindex. 'Is there a women's section of the baths?'

'Of course,' said Vindex.

Juba fished in his belt pouch. 'Ursula, you and Bouda can use the women's part of the baths.' He gave each of them a copper coin.

'How will we find each other after?' asked Fronto as he took his coin.

Juba thought for a moment, then his face lightened. 'Remember we saw all the little altars behind the temple? Let's meet there in no more than two hours. By then I hope to have bought an altar for us to dedicate,' he added, putting up his hood. 'I see a stonemason's stall.'

'Juba! Your hood!' said Fronto.

Juba nodded. 'If it's up it hides my face,' he said. 'And if

I'm on my own they won't think I'm one of the Three Hooded Questers.'

Fronto nodded and made the sign against evil. Then, as the last of the soldiers marched past, he and Vindex fell into step behind them.

As they went through the arch that marked the entry to the sacred area of baths and temple, he was careful to step with his right foot first.

They followed the archers into a bright courtyard dominated by a big square altar and surrounded by lofty marble buildings. Fronto recognised the bath complex. And the tall building on his right had to be the temple of Sulis Minerva, the most important goddess of this place. Four big columns held up the red-tiled roof. And a terrifying face stared out from its triangular pediment.

Fronto stopped so abruptly that the girls bumped into him.

'Fronto!' cried Ursula impatiently.

But he could not reply.

The carved and painted marble showed a face like Medusa's, only this was a male version, with spiky hair, staring eyes and snakes for a beard.

It was the face that had made him run from the Deathwoods.

'Eeeek!' cried Fronto, and he almost wet himself with terror.

Chapter Eight
APODYTERIUM

Fronto was miserable.

Apart from squealing like a girl and nearly wetting himself, the worst thing about seeing the snake-bearded face on the temple roof had been Bouda's look of scorn.

Again.

'Show some courage!' she had hissed.

Now he was muttering the same thing to himself as he and Vindex followed the Syrian archers along a painted corridor into the men's changing room of the baths. 'Show some courage! Show some courage!' he chanted under his breath. '*Right, left, right.*'

But he stopped murmuring as he and Vindex entered the high-domed changing room. He could hear the echoing voices of nearly a hundred men mingled with the clink of armour being laid across benches and hobnail boots being dropped on the tile floor. Once naked, the men passed through a door at the far end of the big changing room, leaving their tunics, shoes, armour and pack-sticks in cubicles and on benches.

'Quickly! Strip off!' said Vindex under his breath. 'So they won't be able to tell that we're not soldiers.'

But before Fronto could even pull off his hooded cloak, a

42

hand came down hard on his shoulder. 'Syrian Scorpions get priority,' growled a brown-skinned soldier, still in his boots and chainmail armour. 'Come back in hour.' He spoke Latin with an accent.

Dejected, Fronto turned away. He had so wanted to immerse himself in the magic waters.

But Vindex stood firm. 'We want to join!' the British boy said boldly, also in Latin. 'We want to be Syrian Scorpions, too.'

Fronto stared at Vindex in astonishment.

'Really?' said the Syrian, a look of amusement on his face.

'Yes!' said Vindex and nudged Fronto with his elbow.

'Yes,' agreed Fronto. He realised Vindex was trying to convince the guard to let them in.

'Well,' said the soldier, 'we *are* looking for new recruits, and you two look old enough. But to enlist you must go to big fortress called Isca Augusta in next few days.'

'Isca Augusta?' said Fronto. 'But that's a legionary fortress, not an auxiliary fort. Auxiliaries don't usually share with legionaries.'

'True,' said the Syrian, 'but lots of their barracks are empty. Our centurion wants us training with proper legionaries, so we spend winter there. If you really want to join, get there in the next few days. Now get out!' He pushed them towards the exit.

'Don't you have to be Syrian to join the Syrian Scorpions?' Fronto asked over his shoulder as the soldier directed them back the way they had come.

'No,' said the Syrian. 'If you have good eyesight and know how to use bow and arrow, then you can join.'

'Who've you got there, Camulus?' asked a stocky man with a hairy chest and back. He was naked but Fronto could tell from his accent and skin colour that he was a Roman from Italia.

The Syrian snapped a salute at the naked Roman. 'Two

would-be recruits,' he said. 'They try to sneak in.'

'Oh, let them in,' laughed the officer. 'These baths are huge. Come on in, lads,' he said. 'Once you've stripped off nobody will look twice. Especially at you,' he said, nodding at Fronto. 'Where are you from anyway?'

'Rome,' said Fronto. 'My grandfather was from Africa and my mother was Italian.'

Too late he remembered the Emperor's edict for their arrest. The Roman was an officer; would he be on the lookout for three brown-skinned children on the run?

But the officer merely nodded and pointed at some small cubicles against the wall. 'Leave your clothes and shoes in those cubicles near ours,' he said. 'Camulus has volunteered to guard our gear. He'll watch yours, too.'

'You aren't bathing?' Vindex asked the Syrian.

'No. Don't like heat,' said Camulus. 'My mother was Thracian and I got her cold blood. That's why I signed up to come to cool Britannia.'

'If my younger brother comes in here,' said Fronto, 'tell him to put his clothes in a cubicle near ours?'

The Syrian saluted Fronto as he had saluted his officer and they all laughed.

Quickly Fronto and Vindex stripped off their clothes, folded them and put them along with their boots in adjoining cubicles on the wall. Then they went through the doorway after the Syrian archers.

A rectangular pool of steaming water lay beneath a lofty vaulted ceiling. A century of Syrian archers were there – eighty men – along with two dozen Romans who must be from the town and perhaps ten wealthy Britons.

They were all naked, but Fronto could still tell them apart.

He could tell the wealthy Britons by their long hair and moustaches, and the gold torcs around their necks.

He could tell the Roman civilians by their short hair, clean-shaven faces and expansive hand gestures.

He could tell the Syrian auxiliaries by their nut-brown skin, muscular bodies and battle scars. One man walked by close enough for Fronto to see a star-shaped pink scar on his shoulder. He shuddered; an arrow must have caused it.

Despite the number of men in the room, it wasn't noisy at all. Sounds of splashing and echoing voices rose up and were lost in the vast ceiling space, now pierced by shafts of golden sunlight slanting down through high windows.

Vindex was watching him with a smile. 'Don't tell me you haven't seen better baths in Rome?' he said.

Fronto realised he was gaping and closed his mouth. 'I've seen many fine baths like this in Rome, but I never expected anything like this in Britannia. Also, there's something different about these baths,' he said. 'Like a presence . . .'

'That's because the goddess lives here. In the hot spring next door. Come on!' Vindex stepped into the pool with barely a splash and stood chin deep in the pale green water. 'It's lovely.'

Fronto went to the edge of the great pool. 'It's lined with lead!' he exclaimed. 'And the water's hot!' he added as he dipped a toe. 'In Rome big swimming pools like this are always cool. It would take a forest to heat a bath this size.'

'This hot water gushes out of the sacred spring,' said Vindex. 'Barrels and barrels of it, every hour!'

Fronto wrinkled his nose. 'It smells like eggs,' he said.

'That's the magic part!' said Vindex. 'Come on!'

Fronto tapped the warm lead lining of the pool – *right, left, right* – and lowered himself in.

It was glorious. The water surrounded and lifted him, warming him from the tips of his toes to the end of his chin.

Suddenly some bubbles rose to the surface and plopped softly.

'What did you do?' Fronto looked at Vindex accusingly.

'It wasn't me,' laughed Vindex. 'It was the goddess. That's her way of speaking. When the water moves it means she's listening; if you have a prayer, make it now.'

Fronto nodded, then closed his eyes and floated on his back. As water filled his ears, the echoing voices of the bath-house faded and he seemed to hear the distant battle horn of a Roman cohort. 'Please, Sulis Minerva,' he prayed, 'make me brave.'

Chapter Nine
FONS SACER

Ursula came out of the bath-house and into the temple courtyard just in time to see blood spurt up from a calf's neck.

She clapped both hands over her mouth, knowing that any sound – and especially a scream – would arouse the rage of the priest bending over the animal and the people who had paid for the sacrifice. That was the point of the flute that was playing softly: to muffle unlucky noises. Now she could smell the blood through the cloud of incense and she moved her right hand up to cover her nostrils.

Bouda rolled her eyes. 'You grew up in Rome; aren't you used to sacrifices?'

Ursula shook her head. 'I was hardly ever allowed out of our villa. My parents only let me go into town on flower market days, with my mother and two bodyguards.'

Bouda stood on tiptoe and shaded her eyes. 'I don't see your brothers anywhere,' she said. 'Let's make an offering at the sacred spring. I want to send a prayer to Sulis Minerva.'

'Where's the sacred spring?' asked Ursula.

'There.' Bouda pointed at some men and women gathered around an irregular pool of greenish water that steamed in the

47

cold morning. 'Come on.' She led the way down the steps.

'What are you going to ask the goddess to give you?' Ursula averted her eyes as they passed the priest cutting open the calf.

'Not what,' said Bouda. 'Whom.'

Ursula was surprised. She was planning to pray for someone, too.

'Who?' asked Ursula.

'Not telling,' said Bouda primly.

They found a space next to each other at a waist-high marble wall.

On Ursula's right was a woman with a Roman-style palla over her head. She was muttering in Latin, 'Oh goddess of the spring: Minerva or Sulis or whoever you are. I, Victoriana, give you the person who stole my necklace, whether slave or free, man or woman, Roman or not. I pray that you drown them in a river unless they return that which they stole.'

The woman opened her hand and dropped something into the steaming water. Ursula caught a glimpse of something like a tiny grey sausage and realised it must be one of the rolled up curse tablets the stallholder had been selling. The woman bowed her head and muttered under her breath, then bent to kiss the marble top of the low wall. As she turned away, Ursula saw that her face was hard and unforgiving.

On Ursula's left, Bouda was fumbling in the cloth bag on a blue cord around her neck. Finally she fished out a coin. Ursula saw a flash of silver and gasped.

Bouda was going to give a whole denarius!

Bouda held the coin over the water and prayed loud enough for Ursula to hear: 'Dear Sulis Minerva, goddess of the sanctuary, please protect the boy I love and make him love me back.'

Ursula stifled another gasp: Bouda was praying for love! It

had to be for Castor, the handsome young owner of the ship that had brought them to Britannia.

Ursula felt her eyes fill with tears. It wasn't fair! She had loved Castor since the moment on board ship when he had called her 'brave' and looked at her with his stormy grey eyes. And now Bouda had got her prayer in first!

What happened if two people prayed the same prayer? Did the goddess listen to the first one? Or did the goddess answer the prayer of the one who paid more? Bouda had dropped a silver denarius in. Ursula couldn't compete with that . . . Or could she?

Ursula waited until Bouda had turned away and a goat-smelling man had taken her place.

Then she leaned on the marble wall and peered over. Down below was the gently bubbling water. She could smell eggs and feel warm steam on her face.

What could she give? All she had were the clothes on her back and a brass dupondius that Juba had given her.

And the ivory Venus down the front of her tunic.

Did she dare drop Venus into the sacred spring?

Could you dedicate one goddess to another? Surely not.

Venus was Ursula's personal goddess and had kept her safe for two months since the night they had escaped from Rome.

Ursula closed her eyes and fished down the front of her tunic. She felt the coin and she felt the statuette. She only hesitated for a moment, then took out her offering.

With her eyes still closed she prayed. 'Please, Sulis Minerva,' she whispered fervently, 'protect Castor, the boy I love, and help me find his long-lost brother so he will love me back!'

She opened her hand and when she heard a soft splash she opened her eyes.

She was about to turn away when she saw something impossible. Standing on the other side of the spring was a boy in a black hooded cloak. As he lifted his head she saw grey eyes beneath straight black eyebrows, a straight nose and a sensitive mouth.

Ursula gasped in delight. Her prayers had brought him to her. 'Castor!' she cried, waving her arm. 'Over here! It's me: Ursula!'

He glanced over curiously, as did a dozen others, but he showed no sign of recognition as she pushed through the crowd towards him.

And by the time she reached the other side of the sacred spring, he was gone.

Chapter Ten
FRICATIO

Naked apart from the Minerva gem around his neck, Juba eased himself into the hot water of the great pool and sighed with relief. Not even in Rome had he stood in a pool of piping hot water right up to his chin. It was magical, and he could feel the healing begin.

His brother must have moved on to the cold plunge or steam room but a laughing group of brown-skinned archers were taking turns diving from a large stone slab at the far end of the pool. Their shouts and splashes drifted up to the lofty vaults and came back to him as dim echoes.

Juba stayed in the hot water as long as he could bear it, going right under three times. At last he came out, dripping and steaming, and wrapped himself in the linen towel they had given him. There were alcoves with couches and one of them was free. He lay down on it and almost immediately a boy of about his age came up with a bottle of oil. 'Massage, sir?'

Juba smiled at being called 'Sir', but nodded and rolled over onto his stomach. The boy poured olive oil on his hands and rubbed Juba's back with strong but gentle strokes.

Juba's eyes suddenly filled with tears. The massage made him think of Rome, and home. And that made him think of his father and mother who had given their lives so that he and his siblings could escape.

His mother's last wish had been for him to save the children. He knew she had meant his brother and sisters, but once in Britannia, that request had taken on a new and deeper meaning.

In Londinium they had met a clever and compassionate Roman lady named Flavia Gemina, who had commissioned them to become Questers of Lost Children. She had promised to be their patroness in their efforts to help other lost children like themselves.

Now, having cashed in just two of the gems in his father's cloak and having bought an altar with a thousand sesterces left over, he was beginning to see a way to look after his brother and sister and help other lost, endangered or kidnapped children.

Again he considered the possibility of building a villa near this Roman-feeling sanctuary so far from Rome. It could have animals and a vegetable garden for Ursula, who loved the country life, but it could also have frescoes and inner courtyards and underfloor heating for Fronto, who missed Rome. Best of all, it could be the perfect base from which to search for missing or kidnapped children. Their encounter with anxious parents on the bridge had shown him that this was a place people came to pray for lost children, and to seek news of them.

A deep sense of peace washed over Juba as the boy's fingers continued to work out the knots in his muscles. He felt warm, relaxed, floating.

For the first time in over two months he allowed his hopes to rise a little.

He even smiled when he thought of the altar that would be waiting for him when he came out. He had found one with the three hooded figures already on it with a space below for a short inscription. He had asked the mason to carve the words *In fulfilment of a vow*. He hoped his brother and sister would appreciate the irony, but also that the altar would appease the mysterious hooded spirits, whoever they might be.

The bath-boy patted Juba's back to signify that he had finished and covered him with a second towel so that he would not get cold.

Juba let himself drift off. It was so relaxed here. So peaceful. So quiet.

Too quiet.

Suddenly he was awake.

The silence told him that the Syrian auxiliaries had gone and with them the dark-skinned man who had promised to guard Juba's cubicle. And everyone knew that thieves loved to prowl the changing rooms in public baths.

'What time is it?' he cried, sitting up. 'How long have I been lying here?'

'No more than an hour, sir,' said the boy, his blue eyes wide. Then, almost apologetically, he added, 'That will be a quadrans for the massage, please.'

Clutching his towel around his waist, Juba ran for the changing room.

His feet almost slipped on the pale gold stone around the great pool but he caught himself and rounded the corner into the high-domed room.

'Please may my cloak be there!' he prayed. 'Please Jupiter, Mercury and Venus, may Father's birrus Britannicus full of gems still be there!'

But when he reached his cubicle he found it was much worse than that. The thief, whoever he was, had taken everything.

Chapter Eleven
AUXILIA

An hour later, Fronto and the others sat at the back of a canvas-covered ox-cart, stunned by Juba's news that his stolen cloak had contained a fortune in jewels.

A bath attendant had found Fronto waiting by the altar with the others. A thief, said the messenger, had taken every scrap of his brother's clothing, including his loincloth.

Now, barefoot and bareheaded, Juba was wearing Fronto's undertunic belted with a plait of rawhide bought at a souvenir stall. Fronto tried to think of something to say to cheer his brother, but he had no words.

Surprisingly, Bouda did.

'My gang boss in Londinium was a cruel tyrant,' she said. 'But he taught me some useful lessons. Whenever something bad happened, he told us to look on the other side of the coin.'

Juba stared bleakly at the road unrolling behind them, so Fronto prompted her.

'What do you mean?' he asked.

'You know how when you flip a coin, heads are lucky and ships are unlucky?'

'They are?' said Fronto. 'I never heard of that.'

'You obviously don't gamble much,' she said with a smile.

'Anyway, it goes like this: on one side of the coin, it's unlucky that Juba's cloak full of gems was stolen,' she said, 'but on the other, it's lucky that he still has the Minerva cameo.'

'Oh, I understand!' said Fronto. 'On one side, it was unlucky that all Juba's money was stolen. On the other side, it was lucky that he paid the priest in advance so we could fulfil our vow and dedicate the altar.'

'Exactly!' said Bouda.

'I've got a two-sided coin for Juba!' said Ursula. 'It was unlucky that Juba fell asleep in the baths making the priest get angry at having to wait for him and making us all late back to the village but it was lucky that Vindex spotted this covered ox-cart heading south.'

'And that I know the driver,' added Vindex. 'Also, it was unlucky that his hooded cloak was stolen, but on the other side of the coin it was lucky because now nobody will recognise him as one of the Three Hooded Questers and worship him to death.'

'See?' said Bouda. 'It works!'

Fronto gazed at her in puzzlement. For the past two weeks she had been grumpy and miserable. And now that they had been robbed of a fortune, she was suddenly cheerful. She had spent some of her own precious money to buy Juba the souvenir belt and had even let him wrap her palla around his shivering shoulders.

Bouda was looking at Juba with bright eyes. 'Does that help at all?' she asked him. They all looked at him.

Juba kept his eyes on the road and shook his head. 'I was going to use the money to buy us a house or even a villa,' he said. 'We could have lived there and used it as a base to rescue children,'

'What do you mean, "rescue children"?' asked Vindex.

Juba took a deep breath. 'It's our calling,' he said. 'We believe the gods want us to save other lost or kidnapped children.'

'Our mother's last words to Juba were "save the children",' Fronto explained.

'And a lady named Flavia Gemina made us an unofficial Guild of Questers,' added Ursula.

'We all have secret names,' said Bouda. 'Mine is Vulpa, which means fox.'

'You can still be Questers,' said Vindex. 'Just make Soft Hill your base of operations. You know you can stay as long as you want. We'll build you a roundhouse of your own if you don't like sleeping with us.'

Juba nodded his thanks. 'That's kind. But we can't stay with you forever.'

'Yes, we can!' said Ursula. 'I love living in the village.'

'No, we can't!' said Fronto. 'I hate living in the village.'

Ursula looked at Fronto in surprise. 'You hate living in Soft Hill?'

He shrugged and then nodded. 'There's no order or symmetry. I miss straight lines and corners. I don't fit in. Don't be offended,' he said to Vindex.

'I'm not offended!' said Vindex. 'I want to get out of there, too. That's why I think we should join the army. The soldiers in the changing rooms even told us how we can enlist!'

'They were just teasing us.' Fronto shifted on the hay at the bottom of the wagon.

'No,' said Vindex. 'I don't think they were.'

Fronto shrugged. 'I'm not old enough.'

'How old are you?' Vindex said.

'I'll be fifteen next month,' said Fronto.

'Me too!' cried Vindex. 'That means we can join! You said

you miss straight lines and corners. There are plenty of those in a legionary fortress. Come with me to Isca Augusta. Let's sign up as auxiliaries. They'll feed us and house us and train us and pay us. If we enlist together, then we might even be bunkmates.' He turned excitedly to Juba. 'You could come, too!'

Juba shook his head. 'I'm definitely too young,' he said. 'Also, I could never be in the army. I hate people telling me what to do.'

'I don't mind people telling me what to do,' said Fronto. 'Especially when they know what they're doing.'

'Then let's join!' cried Vindex. 'What's stopping us? We can go to Abonae, catch the ferry and be there in under a day. We could go tomorrow.'

'Tomorrow?' Fronto gripped the side of the wagon as they went over a bump. He felt unbalanced.

'Yes, tomorrow,' said Vindex. 'Remember they said if we want to enlist we have to do it in the next few days?'

'I can't,' Fronto blurted. 'I can't leave Juba and Ursula.'

'Of course you can,' said Vindex. 'Juba won't mind, will you Juba?'

Juba did not reply. He was still staring out at the road behind them. Then he turned to look at Fronto. 'It was always your plan to join the army. You're fifteen and almost a man. You can join here as easily as in Rome. Don't let the Emperor spoil our lives any more than he already has.'

Fronto pondered this for a moment. 'But what about Flavia Gemina's commission for us to be Questers and look for lost children?' he said.

'You can still do that in the army. In fact, it might be useful to have you there!'

Fronto was surprised at this reaction and tried to think of

another objection. 'As long as Domitian is alive,' he said, 'I can't give my real name.'

'Use your secret Quester name,' said Bouda.

Fronto looked at her in surprise. 'You think I should enlist?'

She nodded. 'You'd get to wear that glittery armour.'

'I think it's a good idea, too,' said Ursula. She leaned forward and whispered in his ear. 'It might help you find your courage . . .'

Fronto's heart was thumping now. There must be another reason to stop him taking such bold action. 'I'd have to join as a raw recruit,' he said. 'Not as an officer.'

Vindex snorted. 'So? Scared of basic training?'

Before Fronto could reply, Juba said, 'Four months of intensive training? Twelve-hour days with only two meals? Forced marches? Hours of sword and spear practice under a centurion who might break his vine stick over your back if you make a tiny mistake? Communal toilets? Of course he's scared!'

For the first time since Juba had told them about the theft, they laughed.

'But think of the advantages!' said Vindex after a few moments. 'If you join the army you become strong and lean. You learn how to fight. You learn how to work as a team. They train you to use a sword, throw a javelin, fire an arrow. They feed you and clothe you and give you shelter. You can drink wine and play dice and wear armour and impress the girls.'

'If I enlisted,' said Fronto, 'it wouldn't be for any of those reasons.'

'No?' said Vindex. They all looked at him.

'No,' said Fronto. 'The thing I always liked about the army is that you have a routine. Everyone has a job. You take orders and you give orders. You always know what you're supposed to be doing and when.'

'Then join!' said Juba. 'Now that we have no money . . .'

It made sense, but the thought of it made his stomach clench. 'Once we sign up,' Fronto said to Vindex, 'we're committed for twenty-five years.'

'Yes, but if we survive, we get a pouch of gold or a plot of land and we can live the rest of our lives in comfort.'

'But we'll be so old! We'll be nearly forty!'

Suddenly, the ox-cart jolted to a halt. 'This is where you get off,' cried the driver from the front.

'It is?' said Bouda, squinting into the dusk.

'Yes.' Vindex pointed. 'That path is the short cut we took from the village.'

As they clambered off the back of the cart, Fronto tried to think of another argument against joining the army.

'Are you sure you wouldn't mind if I left forever?' he asked Juba.

'I promise I won't mind,' said Juba.

'Ursula?' Fronto turned to look at his sister. But Ursula was looking wide-eyed at the top of Soft Hill, just visible above the trees. 'Look!' she gasped.

They all turned to see a plume of smoke rising from the woods right where their village should be.

'Oh no,' muttered Fronto, making the sign against evil. 'The village is on fire!'

Chapter Twelve
INCENDIUM

U rsula couldn't believe what she was seeing.
          'Someone has set the village on fire!' she cried. 'Meer and Loquax are there!'

She pushed past Vindex and charged down the path between the trees, trying not to slip on leaves or trip on treacherous roots. As she burst out of the greenwoods, she saw that the plume of smoke was rising not from the village, but from somewhere in the Deathwoods beyond.

She heaved a sigh of relief and uttered a prayer of thanks to the gods. Then she frowned. The village looked utterly deserted with no smoke rising from the conical thatched roofs. Quickly, she undid the gate in the wattle fence. As she ran towards her roundhouse, the sheep and the goats regarded her placidly through the wooden lattice of their pens.

With a prayer to Venus, she pushed aside the deer-skin that acted as a door flap and entered the dim roundhouse. The central hearth fire had died down to coals and gave only a dim red light. Ursula hurried across the rush-strewn floor to her sleeping place. Loquax was there, in his covered cage, but Meer was nowhere to be seen.

She let Loquax out of his cage and he fluttered around her

head. The light grew a little brighter as the others pushed aside the door flap to come into the roundhouse.

'Nobody's here!' Ursula cried. 'And Meer is gone!'

'*I'm not scared; I'm excited!*' said Loquax, fluttering above her.

'Everyone's in the Deathwoods!' said Vindex. 'You ran away before I could tell you.'

Fronto rounded on Vindex. 'You told me you weren't allowed in the Deathwoods!' he cried.

'Except for a few nights of the year. And tonight is one of them. Tomorrow is our day of the dead so tonight we burn a fire to honour our ancestors. That's where the smoke is coming from.'

Vindex took a birch-bark torch from a stack by the wall and came over to the smouldering hearth fire. He pushed the sticky black end into the flames and when the torch was burning brightly, he went to the door of the roundhouse and held the door flap open. 'Come on,' he said. 'There will be food and drink there. When it gets a little darker they burn a giant made out of woven hazel branches. That's what Bruvix wanted Fronto to see this morning. The hazel man.'

'So you *were* in on it!' Ursula cried.

'Yes,' said Vindex, following them out. 'But only so Bruvix wouldn't pound me.' He turned to Fronto. 'I'm sorry. Really I am. That's one reason I want to join the army. To get away from those bullies.'

'Will someone at the festival have Meer?' cried Ursula, running to the brook.

Without waiting for a reply, she ran across the wobbly log. But once on the other side, she hesitated. The sapphire sky of dusk still gave some light, but the woods were inky black and she was not sure where to enter.

'Wait for me!' cried Vindex. 'It's getting dark and I know the way.'

Ursula hopped up and down with impatience as Loquax fluttered above her head.

Vindex lowered his head and his torch to enter the woods between two oaks.

Ursula followed without hesitation.

And entered a different world. Tatters of mist drifted on the ground and the flickering torchlight made the black oaks seem to move closer. Ursula shivered but she did not hesitate. Her kitten needed her. She could clearly see the path beaten by the villagers and she could hear the faint, rhythmic thump of drums up ahead.

As they went deeper into the Deathwoods, the sound of drums got louder and when they left the twisted oaks behind and started through a sea of dead ferns, she could also hear chanting and shrill flutes. The well-beaten path led past brambles and fallen trunks, one of which had roots like the fingers of a giant hand reaching out for them.

Somewhere up ahead an owl hooted. A moment later she saw it drift past on silent wings and heard a shrew squeal as it was taken.

Loquax flapped up from her shoulder crying, '*Druid in the Deathwoods!*' It was so unexpected that Ursula jumped along with the others.

'Where?' said Fronto. 'Do you see it?'

'There's nobody here,' said Vindex. 'They'll all be in the clearing up ahead.'

After another twenty paces, the woods gave way to a clearing with a huge bonfire burning at its centre.

She could hear laughter and music and dogs barking happily.

She could smell meat on the spit and woodsmoke.

She could see a man woven of branches, twice as tall as the trees, near the blazing bonfire. Smoke billowed up and dark figures danced in front of the yellow flames. Their flapping cloaks made them look like black moths circling a lamphorn. Some of the dancing figures were adults but others were children.

'One of them must have Meer!' she cried, and ran forward.

The brown grass was wet with dew and her boots were soaked by the time she reached the dancing children.

She grabbed the nearest girl by her shoulders. 'Have you seen my kitten?' she cried. But the girl was oblivious. Her eyes were half closed and she was swaying her head.

'*Meeer!*' came a plaintive meow behind her, almost drowned out by the buzzy music and throbbing drums.

Ursula turned with a squeal of delight. 'Meer!'

Meer was clinging to the cloaked shoulder of a girl named Valatta. The girl was twirling in one spot. As Ursula watched, Valatta staggered and almost fell over.

'To me, Meer!' cried Ursula.

The kitten launched herself at her mistress and scrabbled up to her shoulder using her needle-sharp claws.

Before Ursula could kiss her kitten's nose, Valatta had grabbed her hands and was spinning her around.

'*Carpe diem!*' cried Loquax, fluttering up.

'*Meeer!*' said Meer, clinging tight.

Ursula laughed and allowed Valatta to spin her. Now that she knew Meer was safe, she could surrender to the joy of the moment.

Chapter Thirteen
SAMHAIN

Fronto watched the dancers in astonishment.

Some of the villagers had cast off their cloaks. Underneath they were almost naked, their bodies painted with swirls of blue clay. He was shocked to see women dancing as well as men. He felt his face grow hot.

'Seneca calls such festivals orgies of indulgence,' murmured Juba, but his eyes were wide, too.

The dancers were swaying and writhing, and some of them were uttering strange howls and yips.

Then Bouda did something surprising. 'Don't be so pious!' she said, and turned to Juba. 'Come, dance with me!'

Fronto felt a strange twist in his gut as the girl he liked took his brother's hand and pulled him across the brown grass towards the fire. Juba was still wearing the palla Bouda had let him borrow, but as they started to dance near the heat of the fire, he shrugged it off and she took her cape off, too.

Fronto stood watching them for a long time. Presently he was aware of Vindex standing quietly at his side.

Fronto glanced at him. 'Why don't you join them?'

Vindex frowned. 'I celebrated too hard last year. I drank too much beer and was sick all night and can't remember anything. I don't like losing control,' he added.

'Me neither,' said Fronto.

'Also,' said Vindex, 'Bruvix and Bellator usually play some trick on me. Last year they dressed up as bears. That much I remember.'

'If a bear attacks me then I won't run,' said Fronto.

Vindex laughed and Fronto felt a little better.

'Let's get some food,' said Vindex, 'and make sure people see us. Then we can go back to the roundhouse and you can recite more of the *Aeneid*. It's good for my Latin and I want to know what happens next.'

'All right,' said Fronto. 'I am hungry.'

The smell of roast pork led them to a spit on the other side of the fire. Bruvix and Bellator were turning a boar and Velvinnus was using a sharp knife to slice off pieces as people came forward.

'Vindex!' cried Velvinnus. 'How were the waters of the goddess?'

'Good, Grandfather,' said Vindex.

'Did Sulis speak to you?'

'Yes, I think so. I'll tell you tomorrow.'

Velvinnus nodded and gave them both slices of hot meat on warm flatbread.

The two of them retreated to the shadows to watch while they ate.

A skinny old man danced by, wearing the head of a freshly killed stag like a cap. The oozing blood made his grey hair red and dripped down on his white shoulders. Fronto shuddered with disgust. He looked like a monster from mythology: half human and half animal.

There was no order here. Everything was twisted and dark,

like the forest around them. Fronto swallowed his last piece of bread and meat. The drumbeats filled his ears and his head; they made his whole body vibrate. They seemed to be saying *Come to me now and lose yourself.*

The Britons were barbarians.

But so was he.

For the first time it occurred to him that he could be a hero or a monster. A hero was half god, partly divine. A monster was half animal, like the Minotaur. He wanted to be part god, but with the drums throbbing like that, he felt the terrible temptation to give in to his bestial nature. He could go out among them and put out his arms and close his eyes. If he put up the hood of his cloak, nobody could tell who he was.

He gave his head a shake to clear it.

Then, just when he thought it could not get any stranger, several youths with torches ran forward and touched them to the base of the giant man woven out of hazel and hawthorn. The dark shape seemed to come alive as the flames took hold.

It looked like a real man on fire, if a man could stand twice as tall as the trees.

Fronto remembered what Caesar had said about Druids putting men in giant wicker cages and then setting them on fire. He shuddered and looked at Vindex. His friend was scowling at the burning man, his fists clenched by his side. Then Fronto looked at the villagers. They were dancing and whooping, more undignified and wild than ever. Some couples had gone into the woods.

He could not distinguish Ursula from the other girls and he saw Juba and Bouda stagger and fall onto the ground from dizziness. If he stayed in this village perhaps he would give in to his animal side, like them.

Fronto closed his eyes and touched the statue of Jupiter down the front of his tunic. 'Please, Father Jupiter,' he prayed. 'Show me what to do.'

Now the wicker man was roaring, his shape sending off waves of heat. Fronto opened his eyes to see a great orangey-brown plume of smoke and sparks rise up to the stars. The arms were outstretched, like a man on a cross. As he watched, one of the arms slowly collapsed and fell in a shower of sparks. People laughed and jumped back, but to Fronto it seemed the burning man was pointing west with his remaining arm.

'Which direction is the fortress?' Fronto asked Vindex.

'Isca Augusta is that way.' His friend pointed in exactly the same direction as the burning man's arm.

Was this an omen?

Fronto turned to Vindex. 'All right,' he said. 'I'll go with you. We'll join the army together.'

II

Chapter Fourteen
FLUMEN SABRINA

The next morning Fronto was woken by a lament for the dead.

Villagers were gathering outside in the chilly morning air, their long fair hair loose and their woollen tunics unbelted. Many of them still had traces of face paint, for they had not washed.

Strumming sad notes on his harp, Bardus led the chanting villagers down to the green mound across from the Deathwoods.

Fronto came up behind Vindex who was standing a little apart with his long bow in his left hand. 'What's that?' Fronto pointed at the mound.

Vindex turned and looked at him in surprise. 'The ashes of our ancestors are buried there, close to the woods and running water.'

'Will it not be ill-omened for us to set out today?' Fronto asked him.

'No, it's a good day. The roads will be empty and as most people stay in their villages, nobody will recognise one of the Hooded Spirits. And it's better we leave today. We don't want to be too late to enlist. We can mourn our dead as we walk,' he added. 'Have you got your bow and arrows?'

Fronto nodded and lifted a flap of his cloak to show Vindex.

'Good,' said Vindex. 'I'm going to say goodbye to my family. I'll be right back.'

As he left, Ursula, Juba and Bouda arrived. Having been up late the night before, the two girls were still sleepy and tousled. In the bright morning light, Fronto could see that Ursula had the traces of painted blue spirals on her cheeks and Bouda's eyes were bloodshot. Juba wore a fine new cloak.

'Did I tell you I'm going to enlist today?' Fronto asked them.

Juba nodded. 'Let's pray and ask the gods to prosper you on the journey and on your new life as a soldier. But first I want to give you this beaver-skin cloak. Velvinnus gave it to me to replace the stolen one.'

He took off his new cloak and held it out.

Fronto didn't understand at first and just stared at his brother.

'Give me yours as a trade,' said Juba. 'It will remind me of you whenever I wear it.'

'Oh, Juba, that's so kind of you,' said Ursula.

'Beaver fur is worth ten times as much as wool,' added Bouda.

Juba smiled at them. 'I know. He'll need it for all the marching.'

They traded cloaks and Fronto was surprised to find the beaver-skin lighter as well as warmer than his woollen cloak. He didn't usually like physical contact but he gave Juba a quick hug.

Then, with the villagers singing in the background, the four of them bowed their heads and prayed for Fronto to have a safe journey.

'Are you sure you don't mind me going?' Fronto asked them after they had finished their prayers.

'We'll miss you,' Juba said. 'But we're glad that Domitian hasn't stopped you from following your heart's desire.'

Ursula's eyes were full of tears as she gave him a fierce hug. Meer purred on her shoulder.

Fronto turned to Bouda. The early sunlight made her tousled hair glint orange like flame.

Before he could say anything she stepped forward, stood on tiptoe and gave him a quick kiss on the cheek. 'Goodbye, Fronto,' she said. 'I hope you find your destiny.' Then she turned and started back towards the village.

'You're not scared, are you?' Juba said.

Fronto was watching Bouda's retreating back. 'I'm terrified,' he said in a low voice. 'That's why I need to do this.'

When the villagers finished their chants, Vindex came up with his family. Little Velvinna clung to her brother's leg. Everyone in his family was weeping, even his grandfather Velvinnus, chieftain of the village. Only Bruvix watched his younger brother with narrowed eyes. Suddenly Velvinna let go of Vindex's leg and hugged Fronto's leg instead.

'I'll miss you, Fronto!' she cried.

Of all the things said and done so far, that was what brought the tears to his eyes.

'Farewell,' he said in a choked voice. 'May the gods protect you!' He turned before they could see his tears.

But Vindex was weeping openly as they set out along an ancient footpath that headed northwest. 'It's permitted to weep on this day,' he said, his streaming eyes still smiling.

At the crest of a hill, they stopped for a moment to look down into the Deathwoods and part of the clearing where they had burned the wicker man the night before. A thin smear of smoke still rose from the ashes. The faintly sour odour of burnt hazel and damp leaves smelled like grief.

They mourned the dead by telling each other stories

of relatives they had lost. Vindex's father had died of a fever three summers before, and a cousin who had also wanted to join the army died of a festering sickle cut before he could enlist.

Fronto told how his elder brother had died aged seven because he had not touched the lintel and also how his father and mother had died in Rome the night they escaped. 'But I never saw their bodies,' he said. 'And my heart still feels as if they are there waiting for me.' He did not mention the baby sister they had left behind. He hoped she was still alive with her new family in Ostia.

When their footpath brought them to a ridge an hour later, with a view of the main road heading west, they stopped to catch their breath. They put down their bows and sat on a log for a breakfast of bread and cheese. Vindex pointed out a river just beyond the road. 'That river flows to an estuary,' he said. 'At a market town called Abonae, a ferry will take us across to the fortress.'

When they stood up again, Vindex pulled a little deer-horn talisman from the neck of his tunic and kissed it for luck. 'It's a wheel of Taranis,' he explained. 'He's our head god, like your Jupiter.'

Fronto patted the familiar bump just above his belt at the front of his tunic. 'Maybe we Romans aren't so different from you,' he said.

When they reached the road, Vindex grinned. 'Shall we practise marching like soldiers?'

Fronto nodded and began to chant one of the marching songs he had heard.

The chant gave them strength and stamina. They followed the road over hill and down, marching until noon, when they stopped beside the widening river and washed down the last of their cheese and bread with its water.

Fronto felt their luck growing with every step that afternoon, especially when they reached the port of Abonae where the river they had been following flowed into a great estuary.

The cold, brass-coloured sun was low in the west. It shone straight into their eyes as they ran to catch the last ferry across the sparkling expanse of water.

Fronto felt the good luck overflowing as they disembarked within sight of the huge timber fortress and a unit of legionaries returning from some mission.

But all their accumulated luck seemed to vanish into mist when the guard at the gate said they weren't taking on any new recruits and growled that they should 'Go to Hades instead.'

Chapter Fifteen
ISCA AUGUSTA

'What do we do now?' Vindex groaned. 'We can't go back to the village. My brother would mock me to the end of my life.'

'Jupiter, help us,' murmured Fronto. 'Jupiter, help us.' He was touching the edge of a wooden table over and over: *right, left, right.*

The two of them were sitting at the wooden table outside a tavern called The Legionary's Rest. From here they could see the fortress gates, even in the gathering dusk.

'Why so glum?' said the innkeeper as he put down a tray with two bowls of stew, two wooden spoons, two beakers and a jug of steaming wine.

Vindex tipped his head towards the fortress. 'We wanted to enlist,' he said. 'But they turned us away.'

'What, him?' The innkeeper pointed at the fierce guard and laughed. 'Don't worry,' he said. 'He's just a Cerberus.'

Fronto stopped tapping and frowned up at the man. 'Cerberus? Like the three-headed dog who guards the Underworld?'

'That's right.' The man was pouring steaming pink liquid into the two beakers. 'Don't you know that every time you want to cross a threshold into a new life there will be a

Cerberus? Someone or something trying to stop you?'

Fronto and Vindex looked at each other.

'And you should never give up,' said the innkeeper, putting down the jug, 'because the better the world on the other side, the harder it will be to get in. As they say, "Who can measure the benefits of a successful army career?" I did my twenty-five years, and with the money they gave me I bought this tavern. That will be eight asses,' he added. 'Six for the stew and two for the wine. The advice is free.'

'Do you think he's right?' said Vindex.

'I don't know,' said Fronto. 'But I do know that thresholds are important.' He took a mouthful of stew. As well as mutton, it had beans, barley and parsnip. Usually he didn't like mixed-up food, but he was ravenous and it was good. They ate two bowls full each and washed it down with the sweet and spicy wine.

The sun had set and torches now appeared on the walkways above the fortress as Vindex pointed.

'Look!' he said. 'Cerberus is gone. They must have changed the sentries while we were eating.'

Fronto drained his beaker and touched the figurine of Jupiter in his tunic for good luck. 'Shall we try again?'

The replacement sentry greeted them with a smile. 'Hello, young lads,' he said. 'What can I do for you this evening?'

'We want to join one of your auxiliary cohorts,' said Fronto.

'You sure about that? You're not doing this on a dare?' He leaned forward and sniffed their breath. 'Or because you've been drinking?'

'No!' said Vindex. 'We walked for a day to get here.'

'We were only warming ourselves at the tavern because the

previous sentry wouldn't let us in,' explained Fronto.

The new sentry laughed, showing brownish teeth. 'That was Postumus, a grumpy old sod. You did well not to give up. In you go!'

'Just like that?' Fronto frowned. 'Aren't you going to ask us the password?'

'Why would you know the password?' the sentry asked cheerfully. 'You haven't joined yet. Besides,' he added, 'it's not like you're a cohort of soldiers arrived unexpected at night or in the rain.'

'Aren't you going to search us for weapons?'

'I can see you're carrying bow and arrows,' said the sentry.

'Aren't you going to test our knowledge of the Roman army?' Fronto persisted. 'I can give you all the facts and figures. For example,' he took a deep breath, 'a legion is made of ten centuries but although century means a hundred there are only eighty men per century because each century is made up of ten contubernia of eight men each and that's why a century only has eighty men.' He took another breath. 'Then there are six centuries in a cohort and ten cohorts in a legion, but one of those cohorts is a double cohort. The commander of a century is a centurion and his right-hand man is—'

'Stop! Stop! Why are you telling me? I know all that.'

'Then aren't you going to measure our heights and ask our ages and search us for signs that we're runaway slaves?'

'No,' laughed the sentry. 'They'll do all that inside. One of the contubernia is lacking two recruits. I reckon the gods have sent you to us.' He half-turned and pointed. 'Go straight up the street to the building at the end with the torches either side of the door. That's the headquarters, the principia.

Tell the guard you want to enlist. Mind you,' he called after them as they passed through the gate and started up the via praetoria, 'a week from now you may wish I hadn't let you in.'

Chapter Sixteen
OPTIO

'RISE UP AND BE COUNTED!'

The voice brought Fronto out of his sleep so violently that he banged his head on some kind of wooden platform. Where was he? Not in a spacious Belgae roundhouse but in a cramped dark space with straight walls. He was lying on a straw mattress rather than soft furs. In place of the pleasant scent of woodsmoke, he almost choked on the fog-like stench of damp wool, sour sweat and extreme flatulence.

Then he remembered.

He was in an army bunkhouse with seven other men and a slave-boy. He had banged his head on the bottom of the bunk above him.

Dazed, he stared around at the dim, cramped room. Other men were groaning as they rolled out of their beds. The fug in the room was almost overpowering. There were only two small windows for ventilation.

'I SAID GET UP!' blasted a voice from the doorway. 'Today is the first day of twenty-five years of service, if you decide to enlist. And every morning will begin just like this, with the blast of a trumpet at dawn. My name is Quietus,' he added,

'AND AS YOU CAN HEAR, I'M NOT QUIET!'

Fronto groaned as the voice made his head pound.

He and Vindex had been shown to this barracks the night before. The other recruits had shared their bread and cheese and it had seemed rude to refuse their offer of wine to wash it down. But Fronto could not even remember going to bed.

'Vindex?' he said groggily, looking around.

'Up here!'

Fronto stood up to see his friend sitting cross-legged on the upper bunk, his tousled blond head in his hands. He noticed Vindex's bow and arrows on the mattress next to the wall.

Fronto's heart leapt. Where were his own bow and arrows? He looked underneath his bunk and breathed a sigh of relief.

'I SAID OUT!' blasted Quietus from the doorway. He wore a helmet with two white feathers, one sticking up over each earflap. It made him look like a fierce owl. He also held a wooden staff as tall as himself with an apple-sized knob on top. 'Empty your bladders and leave your cloaks,' he added in an almost normal voice.

'But it's raining!' protested one boy.

'WHAT ARE YOU? A BUNCH OF LITTLE GIRLS?' Without waiting for an answer he stalked out.

Fronto left his beaver-skin cloak covering his statuette of Jupiter. Then he waited his turn to use a clay chamber pot in the anteroom. A thin slave handed them each a bowl of lukewarm porridge. At last they were outside. A chilly drizzle came from the grey sky. The others were huddled beneath the overhang of a columned porch along with a similar group of youths from the bunkhouse next to theirs. Two-feathered Quietus beckoned them out from their shelter and into the rain.

'FALL IN!' he commanded. 'Two abreast!' Holding his staff,

he led the way along a path between the two rows of barracks with their continuous columned porches.

After a few paces he turned to face them, walking backwards.

'I am an optio,' he said. 'I am the centurion's second-in-command. I am also your best friend because I will tell you how things work. This,' he made a vague circle with his staff, 'is the fortress of Isca Augusta, home of the Second Legion. Those,' he gestured towards men gathering under the porches in front of the bunkhouse doors, 'are your basic Roman legionaries. Best soldiers in the world. Some of you will join them, and others might join an auxiliary unit that is wintering here. There is no shame in becoming an auxiliary. Did you know that in this province auxiliary units outnumber the legionaries by three to one? There are also some cavalry here, as you can smell when the wind is from the north.'

Quietus turned round and faced forward again. They were now passing some dusky-skinned men with dark-slanting eyes. The scents wafting from their breakfasts were exotic and spicy.

Fronto whispered to Vindex, 'Those are the Syrians from Aquae Sulis.'

Quietus pointed at the dusky-skinned men with his knob-headed staff. 'Here you have our new demi-cohort from Syria,' he blared. 'All of them are archers and some of them are horsemen. They often take messages and go on scouting missions. We're hoping to build up the number to a full cohort of five hundred, but their commander is choosy about new blood. If you're not a Roman citizen and can't try as a legionary, you could do worse than a posting with the First Cohort of Hamians.'

The men behind Fronto were murmuring with excitement and he heard a voice say, 'I've come four days' walk to try for the Syrian Scorpions!'

'SILENCE!' blasted Quietus. 'Over the next few months,' he continued, 'we will train you to become part of a great fighting machine. Your training will include marching, learning to use a sword, marching, learning to throw a pilum, marching and more marching. We will also teach you to swim, ride and fire an arrow. But the most important thing that you will learn is . . .?'

'Marching?' suggested Vindex.

'LEARNING TO FOLLOW ORDERS!'

They emerged from the rows of barracks and turned left then right along the via sagularis, a wide road bordered by stables on their right and the high fortress wall on their left. Fronto could see sentries pacing along a walkway high above.

Quietus led them to the left and they exited the southwest gate of the fortress before turning right through a portico with columns on four sides which surrounded a vast rectangle of mud strewn with straw. At either end were wooden posts bearing the scars of many blunt strikes.

'THIS IS YOUR DRILL GROUND,' blared Quietus. 'And here comes your centurion. When he addresses you be sure to say "Sir" with every response. Otherwise I'll smack you on the head with my big stick. Got it?'

'Yes, sir!' they all said.

'When I say *intente*, you will all stand as tall as you can in a nice row with eyes front. *INTENTE!*'

Fronto and the others stood as ordered. Now that they were all together, he could see there were four groups of eight, making thirty-two recruits.

Quietus the owl-feathered optio stepped back as a big soldier with a side-to-side crest on his helmet and a short twisty stick in his hand began to walk up and down in front of them. The optio had told them to keep their eyes facing forward, but he could not take his eyes off the centurion.

He was the ugliest man Fronto had ever seen.

Chapter Seventeen
CENTURIO

The centurion had beady eyes, jutting brows and a massive chin. A pink scar wormed its way from the top of his left eyebrow to the bottom right corner of his mouth.

'What have you brought me this morning, Quietus?' he asked the optio.

'BUNCH OF LITTLE GIRLS, SIR!'

The ugly man grinned, revealing three missing teeth. 'My name is Cicatrix,' he bellowed. 'I am a centurion. You can tell that because the crest on my helmet goes this way. My optio has just informed me that you are a bunch of little girls!' He slapped his vine stick against his metal leg guard. 'But I think you are babies. I'll bet some of you don't even know left from right. *Dextrorsum vertite!*' he commanded.

Fronto turned to the right. So did most of the other recruits. But a rabbit-toothed boy on the end had turned left, so that he and Fronto were facing each other.

'Just as I thought!' the centurion growled. 'You are BABIES!'

Cicatrix's face loomed into view as he blasted the boy facing Fronto.

'You!' he bellowed. 'Which hand do you eat with?'

'This hand, sir!' the boy held up his right hand.

'And which hand do you use to wipe your bottom?'

The boy flushed. 'This hand, sir.' He held up his left.

'At least you know that much,' the centurion muttered. He continued in a louder voice. 'Whenever I say anything with dex, it's to do with the same side as your eating hand. When I say sinister, turn to the bottom-wiping hand. And when I say retrorsum, do an about face. Just you: *Retrorsum!*'

Rabbit-tooth turned so he had his back to Fronto.

'Now march!' yelled Cicatrix. 'Right, left, right! *Dexter, sinister, dexter!* Dex, sin, dex!'

The thirty-two of them marched up and down in the drizzle for a few minutes, making the muddy drill ground even muddier.

From the corner of his eye, Fronto saw other soldiers training.

Some were hacking at the posts with wooden swords. Others were throwing leather-tipped javelins at each other, using heavy wicker shields to deflect them.

Most were dressed in segmented armour over woollen tunics. They had helmets on their heads and sturdy leather caligae over socks on their feet. But he also saw a squad of the brown-skinned archers in their scaled armour over longer tunics.

'When do we get our armour?' he asked the boy in front of him.

The boy turned his head a little. 'You're asking me? The one who doesn't know his left from his right?'

'You get your armour when you get your pay and you get your pay as soon as you take the oath,' blasted Cicatrix. '*Consistite!* Halt!'

They all stopped.

'*Sinistrorsum vertite!*'

They all turned to the left.

'*Intente!*'

They came to attention.

'Pathetic bunch of little girls,' said Cicatrix. He walked slowly up the line, looking at each of them. He prodded them with his vine staff, getting one to lift his chin and another to suck in his stomach.

'Now usually,' he said, 'the Roman army signs you up and gives you your first year's wages the moment you step through that gate. Sometimes even before, if you sign up at one of our recruiting stations. But there have been quite a few deserters recently. Some babies decide not to carry on after all. Too much marching. Or they miss their mummy. So they leave.'

Cicatrix looked at each of them in turn, his beady eyes glittering. 'Do you know what they do to deserters? To little girls who run away?'

Fronto thought he knew the answer but he was too afraid to say. And nobody else dared to speak.

'*Dextrorsum vertite!*' barked Cicatrix and proceeded to march them out of the parade ground to the cemetery beyond. Lying on a bier ready to be put to the flames was the body of a man wearing only a loin-cloth.

Cicatrix had them march past, stop, turn to face the corpse and stand to attention.

'When you desert,' the centurion pointed his vine-stick at the dead man, 'they get your own bunkmates to beat you to death. That is what happened to poor Gaius there.' Cicatrix lowered his vine-stick and looked at each of them in turn. His gaze seemed to linger on Fronto's face as he added, 'So if any of you are having second thoughts, now is the time to run back to mummy.'

Chapter Eighteen
SIGNACULUM

An hour later Fronto and thirty-one other new recruits marched through a vast columned forecourt and through two arches to halt before a room with red and yellow walls. Guarded by two soldiers, the shrine contained a statue of the Emperor flanked by banners and standards, one of which had a golden eagle perched on top.

'This,' said Cicatrix, gesturing around them, 'is the principia. And this shrine,' he pointed at the red and gold room, 'sits at the heart of the fortress. When you first came in through the gate you probably looked ahead through these open doors and saw that gilded eagle. It is the symbol of Rome.'

Fronto felt a swell of pride in his chest.

'You can see the eagle is standing above a banner with a Capricorn embroidered on it. We call ourselves Augusta after the Divine Emperor Augustus. You must be prepared to lay down your lives to protect this eagle, if necessary.'

Fronto's glance strayed to the statue of the Emperor Domitian, the man who wanted him dead. He forced himself to look back at the eagle.

'Before you take the oath,' said Cicatrix, 'I am going to give you one last chance to walk away. First, let me remind you of the benefits of joining the army. You will be looked after for the rest of your life. We will feed you, clothe you, train you and pay you two hundred sesterces a year. That amount will increase if you have a special skill or if you rise to be an officer. Then, after you have served twenty-five years, we will make you a Roman citizen and give you a plot of land or a sum of money.'

Excited whispers ran among the recruits.

Thwack!

The centurion's vine staff smacking against his metal-covered leg commanded instant silence.

'But,' he blared, 'here is my warning. Over the next few months I am going to drive you like a slave driver!' He strode up and down in front of them. 'You lot are as soft as maggots. I am going to make you as hard as rocks. You will become a centipede with a thousand legs, marching, marching, marching. You will become a tortoise, using your shields to cover your heads. You will become a bull, standing firm with a mighty forehead and spears like horns to charge the enemy. In short, you will be a part of the eagle.' Here he pointed to an eagle disc on his breastplate. 'Some of you will be eyes, some talons, some the beak. Most of you will be feathers, working together to make the legion fly. But think of feathers not of fluff but of bronze. Do you understand?'

'Yes, sir!'

'Are you still ready to take the oath?'

'Yes, sir!' they all replied.

'The oath,' he said, gesturing at the standards, 'is a sacred vow. Never to be broken. On pain of death at the hands of your comrades. Do you understand?'

'Yes, sir!' they cried as one.

'If, at any time during this oath you want to leave, this is your last chance. Do you understand?'

'Yes, sir!'

'Recruit number one. Step forward!'

The rabbit-toothed boy stepped forward.

'Raise your right hand!' blared the centurion, and added, 'That's the one you eat with.'

'Yes, sir.'

'Repeat after me: *I swear . . .*'

'I swear . . .'

'*That I will faithfully execute . . .*'

'That I will faithfully execute . . .'

'*All that my officers command.*'

'All that my officers command.'

'*I will never desert the service . . .*'

'I will never desert the service . . .'

'*And I will not shirk death.*'

'And I will not shirk death.'

'*For the sake of Rome and the Emperor.*'

'For the sake of Rome and the Emperor.'

'Good,' said Cicatix. 'Now go one door along to the clerk's office to collect your temporary signaculum.' He pointed to a door to the right of the shrine. 'Then go to that room on the left and collect your pay. Then go to the armoury, and buy your armour. When you have done all those things, you may go to the baths. We have the finest baths this side of the estuary. Bigger than the baths at Aquae Sulis even. After a good steam, I suggest you get your hair shorn. If you have any time after that you can take the rest of the afternoon off. It might be your last free hours for the next six months.' Cicatrix took a deep breath. 'Recruit number two,' he barked, 'step forward!'

Fronto stepped forward, his heart thumping.

'No need to repeat the whole thing,' said Cicatrix. 'If you

agree to abide by the oath then hold up your hand and say idem in me!'

'Idem in me!' said Fronto.

As he followed the rabbit-toothed boy to the clerk's office he heard Vindex say, 'Idem in me!' behind him.

In contrast to the glowing torchlit walls of the shrine, the walls of the clerk's office were pale blue. Combined with pearly light flooding through big windows, it made the room seem chilly.

Fronto shivered when he came in. He saw Rabbit-tooth standing to attention before a table where a plump man sat writing beside a thin man.

'Strip off,' said the plump clerk without looking up. 'We need to note any moles, scars or other distinguishing marks so that we can identify your corpse on the battlefield, if necessary. But first, tell me your name and where you are from so my scribe can make your temporary signaculum.'

'My name is Aelius Clemens,' said the youth as he stripped off. 'My father was a soldier and my mother was of the Iceni tribe.'

As the thin man began inscribing this information on a thin square of lead, Fronto glanced at Vindex behind him.

'What's the matter?' said Vindex with a wink. 'Are you afraid to strip off?'

'No,' said Fronto under his breath. 'I'm just not sure what name to give.'

'What do you mean?'

'I can't give my real name because of the imperial warrant out for my arrest.'

'I thought you had a false name ready to give,' whispered Vindex.

'I do. The wife of the governor's scribe gave it to me: Lucius Flavius Latinus.'

'So call yourself that.'

'I don't think she knew I was going to join the army,' he said. 'What if the Emperor's men find me out? That name might lead back to her. Also, we never came up with a story to go behind it.'

Rabbit-tooth had finished and was pulling on his tunics.

'It's nearly your turn!' hissed Vindex, as the scribe handed Rabbit-tooth his tag. 'Just choose the story of somebody who does not come from your town.'

Fronto felt the familiar taste of sour panic.

Why hadn't he thought this out? Why?

'Next,' said the plump clerk to Fronto. 'Strip off and tell me your name.'

Fronto pulled off his tunics. He was glad he had left his statue of Jupiter in the bunkhouse.

'No distinguishing marks,' the clerk remarked to the scribe, 'apart from his brown skin. I'd guess one parent is from Africa?'

'Yes, sir,' said Fronto. 'My name is . . . he looked desperately around the room. 'Mensa. My name is Mensa.'

'Your name is "Table"?'

'Yes, sir. Julius Mensa. My mother Julia gave birth to me on a table.'

The clerk tried – and failed –to suppress a smile. 'Where are you from, Julius Mensa?'

'From Ostia, sir. I came to Britannia to seek Fortuna's favour.'

'Well I hope you find it. Collect your temporary signaculum from the scribe and don't lose it. Next!'

Chapter Nineteen
NOMINA

The next day Fronto and other recruits stood shorn and shaved and wearing their new armour, bought with their first pay.

Already the exercise ground looked familiar to Fronto, especially as it was drizzling again.

Cicatrix the centurion started them by jogging around the ground in full kit.

'THE POINT OF THIS,' blasted Quietus the optio as he jogged beside them, 'is to see where your armour rubs. You might need to adjust your scarf or get an extra pair of socks. Or you might need to get someone to loosen the stays on the back of your lorica segmentata. Those of you who invested in chain mail, well done. That is my personal favourite. Those of you who want fancy fish-scale armour must wait until the Syrian Scorpions accept you into their cohort.'

Although it was drizzling, Fronto barely noticed. Dressed in a new padded undertunic, his woollen overtunic and a heavy chain mail shirt, along with a felt skullcap under his helmet, he was soon sweating. The cool rain was welcome on his face whenever they had a short break.

After three more laps around the exercise area they were each given a heavy wooden sword and the centurion showed them how to hold it. They chopped and slashed at wooden posts until blisters began to form. Then they jogged some more.

At the sixth hour they broke for hard tack and a cup of hot spiced wine in the muddy exercise area.

'This afternoon,' announced Cicatrix, 'we are going to play Romans and Barbarians.' He pointed at Fronto's bunkmates and the eight men from the barracks next to them. 'You two contubernia are going to be the Romans. Put your swords and daggers on the bench under the colonnade,' he added. 'And take some of those safety swords or a spear with the padded tip, along with a shield.'

He turned to the remaining sixteen recruits. 'You lot, strip down to your breeches. There's a pile of leggings on that bench if you don't wear undergarments. You're going to be the barbarians. You get a shield plus a spear or sword.'

For the next half hour, the 'barbarians' could charge however they liked, but the 'Romans' had to advance in a rank, each man's shield covering his left side and the right of the man on his left.

'My shield arm aches like Hades,' muttered a pink-cheeked boy with dimples. 'I don't think I can keep this up much longer.'

'These shields may be wicker,' said Fronto. 'But they're heavier than the real shields. Same with the swords. So when we get the real thing it will seem easy.'

'My arm feels like it's on fire,' groaned Vindex as they lifted their practice shields slowly to bash the faces of the recruits standing in for barbarians.

'That's it!' bellowed Cicatrix. 'Aim the boss of your shield for their grinning mouths and see if you can break their teeth!

SLOWLY!' he screamed, as one of the 'barbarians' reeled back with a cry. 'This is practice!'

He went to the recruit, heaved him to his feet, had a quick look in his bloody mouth and pushed him cheerfully back into the line.

'Do it again,' he commanded, 'and notice how you can bring the point of your sword up in that space underneath and push it right up into his guts. SLOWLY!' he bellowed again. 'In a moment you lot are going to trade places and your roles will be reversed.'

'What if your opponent is wearing armour, sir?' asked Fronto as he and his bunkmates stripped to be barbarians. 'Won't it protect him against your sword's thrust?'

'Good question!' said Cicatrix. 'At that close range and with all your juices flowing, you should be able to punch your sword through mail or scales or lorica segmentata. If you have kept it clean, sharp and oiled,' he added.

'Do we have to go barefoot, sir?' asked Fronto.

'Yes! Dressing like a barbarian will give you useful insight into his strengths and weaknesses.' He looked at the recruits who had been playing barbarians. 'Had any insight?'

One of the men nodded. 'A half-naked barbarian can move faster than a man in armour,' he said, 'but he's not as well protected.'

'Like gladiators!' cried Fronto. 'The murmillo is heavily armoured but he gets tired more easily than the retiarius with his net and trident.'

'Excellent, Fronto!' said the centurion.

Fronto felt the warm glow of praise. Then his smile faded, and he stood with one sock on and one sock off.

The centurion had called him by his real name!

'What did you call me, sir?'

Cicatrix rolled his eyes. 'Listen,' he said, 'Half of you are Marcus or Gaius or Cuno. I'll learn your names eventually, but I always give my new recruits nicknames.' He nodded at Fronto. 'With your helmet off I can see you have a nice broad forehead. Hence the name.'

Beside him Vindex chuckled. 'You chose a new name and he gave you back your real one!'

'You're Flavus!' the centurion bellowed at Vindex. 'Because you're blond.' He jabbed his stubby finger at two more recruits. 'You're Gelasinus on account of your dimples and you can be Socrates on account of you're old.'

'I'm not old,' lisped the man. 'I'm only thirty-one.'

'That's old for a recruit.' Cicatrix pointed to the rabbit-toothed boy. 'You're Brocchus on account of your rabbit teeth.'

All the recruits were staring now. 'You are Vatia because your knees knock together and you are Varro on account of your knees go out,' he said to the next two.

A few men grumbled at the nicknames Cicatrix had given them and one almost cried when the centurion could not think of a nickname and asked his real name. But most of them were pleased and joked with their friends.

They continued drilling until an hour before dusk, when the trumpet blew the seven most beautiful notes Fronto had ever heard, the signal for end of drills.

Later that night, Fronto lay on his prickly straw mattress.

Every muscle in his body ached. He had blisters on his hands and bruises on his legs and a swollen left eye where he had banged it on his own shield. He was more exhausted than he had ever been in his life.

But for the first time since he had left Rome, he felt at home.

Chapter Twenty
SAGITTARII

Fronto met Hamianus the Archer on the first day of the new year.

Days of training had become weeks and before he knew it, two months had passed.

The Kalends of Januarius dawned bright and cold, with a glazing of frost that made the red roof tiles of the barracks pink and turned the muddy road the colour of nutmeg.

The thirty-two recruits had been told to bring their own bows if they had them. Fronto brought out the beautiful composite bow that Dallara had given him. He had not yet used it and he was excited to try it out.

Vindex had his long bow, just like the one Fronto had dropped in the Deathwoods two months before.

Instead of turning right out of the southwest gate, they turned left towards the amphitheatre. Fronto had been here for some of the Saturnalia celebrations – a small beast hunt and friendly gladiatorial combats between auxiliary cohorts – but today it was deserted, with only some bales of hay for targets at one end.

As they got closer, they saw a brown-faced man with bow and arrows standing beside Cicatrix. Fish-scale armour of yellow brass glittered over a long sage-green tunic. On his head he wore a cone-shaped helmet of silver and bronze with a brass fish-scale neck-guard and a single white feather drooping from its apex.

'This man in the fine helmet is Titus Flavius Hamianus!' announced Cicatrix. 'He is the best archer in the world and he is going to be teaching you little girls how to fire an arrow. He wants to see how many of you have the skill to join the Syrian cohort.'

Hamianus removed his conical helmet to reveal a long face with a smiling mouth, thin nose, pale brown eyes and quizzical eyebrows.

'Good morning,' he said with a smile. His voice was soft and his Latin was good, with only a slight accent. 'Today you will learn how to be best archers in the world.'

He pointed to a row of hay bales each with a bow on it. 'In a moment you will stand behind those hays and fire at those hays.' Here he pointed at the double bales. 'Each one of those represents a man. The ox-skull is being the head. In a few moments we will be firing our arrows at them. But first, let me show you types of arrows you can use.'

Hamianus brought seven arrows out of his quiver and laid them reverently on a bale of golden hay. The Syrian's long eyelashes and sticky-out ears reminded Fronto of a camel he had once seen in Rome.

'This first one,' said Hamianus in a soft voice, 'is your normal hunting head. You can see it is shaped like a leaf with sharp V point. It goes into the body and causes the blood to flow. It comes out clean and sometimes can be stitched and healed. But mostly causes slow death for man or animal. Very bad. Very bad.'

He put it down and picked up the next one. 'This is also a

very bad arrowhead,' he said. 'This one has barbs so that if you pull it out it takes out much flesh. Very painful. Very deadly. This,' here he held up a third, 'has barb attached by sinew to shaft. When you pull it out the head stays in the body. This is especially bad for poisoned arrows.'

'You use poison?' asked Gelasinus, the boy with dimples.

'QUIET IN THE RANKS!' commanded Quietus, his breath puffing white in the cold morning.

But Hamianus nodded solemnly at Gelasinus. 'Some poisons very bad. But we do not use poison. This is not the Roman way.'

'This is worst arrow for men,' said Hamianus picking up the fourth shaft. 'It is called trilobate. You can see it has three blades. This makes most bad wound. You pull out half the man's insides when you remove it. Also it is almost impossible to stitch. Very bad. Very bad.'

Fronto was not the only recruit to make the sign against evil.

'Next we have Roman arrow. This is called Acus. It was invented by tribes in Germania but as Romans win the battles they call it "Roman". This is designed to go through armour. All sorts of lorica, this will pierce. Even my fine squamata, of which I am very proud.'

He looked down at his brass, fish-scale armour and then gave them a radiant smile.

Next he showed them a strange arrow whose iron head was shaped like a half circle. The curved edge was attached to the shaft so that the two cut-off flat edges would strike its victim.

'This is a horse arrow,' said Hamianus. 'It also is very bad. It will stop a charging horse in his tracks. Imagine now a cavalry charge coming at you. Now imagine archers fire a hundred of these arrows. You will stop cavalry charge like horses hitting brick wall. Very bad for them. Very good for us.

'And finally you have your fire arrow. You can see it is like the hollow bud of an iron flower but with most sharp point.' He held up the shaft so they could see that its budlike point contained something brown.

'You put things such as hemp or bitumen or birch bark inside,' explained the Syrian. 'Then light it and shoot it. You can set things on fire and you can also use it for signals. Different plants or oils give different coloured smoke. Look!'

Hamianus flipped open the lid of a cow's horn at his belt and placed the arrow inside. When he pulled it out, the brown material was smoking, as if by magic.

'This is my tinder-horn,' said Hamianus with a gentle smile. 'You can carry small embers for short time, up to an hour or two. But you must pack it carefully.' He blew gently on the stuffed arrowhead until sparks appeared and the wisp of smoke became a plume.

'Now,' he said. 'You must not shoot it too fast, or wind will put out the flame. You must judge perfectly.'

Here he pulled back the string on his bow a little more than halfway, pointed it up and fired it straight up into the air.

Fronto's head tipped back as he and the other men watched the smoking arrow climb higher and higher. When it had almost reached the top of its ascent there was a burst of red and the smoke billowed white.

Everyone gasped, including Quietus and Cicatrix.

When the arrow fell and buried itself halfway between barrier bales and the target bales, all the men applauded.

'QUIET!' bellowed Quietus, but his voice held no conviction.

Hamianus had already lit another fire arrow. Now he took aim at the central bale of hay. For a moment all was silent as they watched the smoking arrow describe a lazy curve before striking the ox-skull that represented the head on one of the target bales. The ox-head exploded and a moment later the hay burst into flame and crackled merrily.

Fronto and all the other recruits cheered.

This time Quietus did not tell them to be quiet. He was cheering, too.

Chapter Twenty-One
BARDUS

For Ursula the winter days fell into a rhythm of waking up with the sun, bringing water from the brook, tending the animals, grinding grain, baking flatbread, eating flatbread and having Latin lessons with Juba who was teaching Latin language in the mornings and reading and writing in the afternoons. Every evening finished with a communal meal and the bard telling stories by the flickering light of the central hearth fire.

Realising that Bouda resented their fame, Juba had told the bard that she was Boudica's great-granddaughter. Now Bardus told stories of how the fierce copper-haired queen had almost led some northern tribes to victory against the Romans. Ursula didn't mind that the villagers had now turned their attention to Bouda; as long as she could spend time with animals she was happy.

Whenever the bard sang his stories, he sat in the most beautiful chair in the village. More like a throne than a chair, it was carved of some dark exotic wood with faces of men and animals hidden in the swirling tendrils. During the day, when not in use, Velvinnus put the Bardic Throne against one of the curving walls by the door.

The village girls had taken to meeting by this chair to grind grain every morning. They brought small bags of grain and their hand mills and sat in a semi-circle around the throne. Six of them would grind while one would sit on the chair and tell stories.

Whenever it was Ursula's turn to sit on the Bardic Throne, she would tell them a story from Homer or Virgil. But one day early in April, she started to tell them the story of her sea voyage from Italia to Britannia.

As soon as she described Castor – the handsome young owner of the merchant ship *Centaur* – all the girls stopped grinding and demanded to hear more about him. Their eyes were wide as she described his glossy black hair, stormy grey eyes and perfect mouth.

When she told how he had saved her kitten Meer, aged only ten days, and barely able to open her eyes, all the girls went 'Ahhh!'

'Even though he saved my kitten, he was very arrogant and cruel,' Ursula said. 'Later that morning he had Juba whipped for not following an order.'

The girls looked at each other with shocked faces.

'Like you would whip a slave?' breathed Valatta.

Ursula nodded. 'While the rest of us worked hard to sail the ship and keep it clean, arrogant Castor stayed in his cabin reading strange scrolls,' she told them. 'Or he would go to the prow and stare longingly ahead. After five weeks of this, Juba and Fronto and I decided we'd had enough. We devised a plot for revenge.'

The girls had stopped grinding again and were staring at Ursula wide-eyed.

'It was Juba's job to empty Castor's chamber pot every morning—'

'A chamber pot?' One of the girls looked puzzled.

'Yes,' said Ursula. 'It's a pot for peeing in.'

'Oh!' they said in unison.

'We decided to balance his own full chamber pot on his half-open door so it would fall on his head.'

'No!' cried the girls and some of them covered their mouths.

'Yes!' said Ursula. Then she lowered her voice dramatically as the storyteller sometimes did. 'So the next time he went to the front of the ship to gaze longingly at the horizon, I went up to distract him while Fronto and Juba put the basin in place. It was the first time in five weeks that I had spoken to Castor. And do you know what?'

They all shook their heads, rapt.

'He was nice to me! He said he had only been hard on us to make us strong for Britannia because when we first came on board we were plump and feeble. We were used to our slaves doing everything for us. But after five weeks we were lean and strong and could speak basic Brittonic.'

'So your time on board the ship was like training!' said Valatta.

Ursula nodded. 'Then he told me he was an orphan.'

'Oh!' said the girls, and their eyes welled up with tears.

'He told me he was travelling to Britannia to find his brother who had been stolen by pirates when he was a tiny baby . . .'

'Oh!' said the girls again. Some of their tears spilled out.

'He apologised for having Juba caned and explained that he had been angry at us because we had paid for our passage by selling our baby sister.'

'What?' They all gazed up at her, mouths agape.

Bouda gasped. 'You sold your baby sister to pay for your passage to Britannia? You never told me that!'

Ursula nodded and her eyes filled with tears. 'One day we'll go back for Dora,' she said, 'but at the time it was the only thing Juba could do.'

The girls ground their grain in silence for a few moments, then Bouda cocked her head to one side. 'So from Castor's point of view,' she said, 'you three were pampered, plump and cowardly. He probably thought he was doing you a favour by being strict with you.'

'Yes. I suppose so.'

'And then he forgave you and was nice to you!'

Ursula nodded.

'Just as you were about to play a terrible prank on him.'

'Yes,' said Ursula.

'Tell us what happened next!' they cried.

Ursula smiled. 'You've finished grinding for today, so I'll tell you tomorrow!'

Bouda raised her voice above their protests. 'I have stories about him, too,' she said. 'Tomorrow or the next day I'll tell you how Castor's beautiful face saved me from a life of crime.'

So it happened that every morning that week, when the girls gathered to grind flour, Ursula or Bouda sat on the Bardic Throne and told them about Castor. The girls learned about his endearing half-smile and how he raised his eyebrows. They knew that when he was worried or thinking hard, he would nibble his thumbnail. And that when he came to a decision he would toss the hair out of his eyes.

When the other village children heard about these stories, they came to listen too, and they made Ursula and Bouda take turns on the Bardic Throne. Soon families from the other houses and even nearby villages were coming to hear the exploits of the mysterious young Roman searching for his brother.

Castor became so famous that when he rode into Soft Hill near the end of April, they all recognised him at once.

Chapter Twenty-Two
NARCISSI

Juba was the only one at Soft Hill not delighted by Castor's arrival.

The tender skin of his waist still twinged sometimes at a place below his right lower rib, a painful reminder of the beating Castor had ordered their first day on board his ship.

It also annoyed Juba that all the girls swooned for Castor like nymphs for Narcissus. Bouda was one of the few who didn't seem in awe of him, but he knew she hid her feelings well.

For a day and a night the villagers feasted Castor. His story had become even more popular than that of the Three Hooded Questers or Boudica's Revolt, which they now knew by heart. The villagers brought him gifts of food and clothing, and Velvinnus had presented him with an iron dagger.

Two days after his arrival Juba, Ursula and Bouda finally found a chance to speak to Castor alone. The four of them went into a sunny clearing full of daffodils in the Green Woods.

'How did you find us?' Juba asked. 'Only one person knows we're here: our patroness.'

'First answer me this,' said Castor. 'What on earth have you been telling them about me?'

Juba looked pointedly at his sister. 'Don't ask me, ask her.'

Ursula gave Castor a sheepish smile. 'I told them that you were looking for your brother who was captured by pirates in infancy.'

Castor snorted. 'I never said it was pirates. But I admit that was the purpose of my coming here to Britannia, to find my brother.'

'Have you had any luck?' Ursula asked him.

'No. But I have found my cousin. She lives in Londinium and her name is Flavia Gemina. I think you have met her.'

Juba looked up. 'Flavia Gemina is your cousin? She's our patroness!'

'I know,' said Castor. 'That's why I'm here. She sent me to see how you are doing.' He glanced around and lowered his voice. 'And to ask you if you have heard anything about Druids.'

'Druids?'

'Yes, there have been rumours of a Druid-led uprising near Lactodurum in the borderland of the Dubonni and Catuvellauni, near the site of Boudica's defeat over thirty years ago. Do you know anything about that?'

Juba frowned and shook his head. 'Fronto thought he saw a Druid in the woods,' he said, 'but that was almost half a year ago, just after we first arrived.'

'I think he imagined it,' said Bouda.

'I think he really saw something,' said Ursula.

'But no definite sightings? Or rumours of an uprising?' Castor was nibbling his thumbnail.

'No,' said Juba. 'But whenever someone's son or daughter goes missing, they blame it on Druids.'

Castor looked up. 'Children have been going missing?'

'Not so much children as young people our age. Or a little older.'

'Flavia Gemina says she appointed you to be her Questers?'

'That's right,' said Juba.

'And have you been Questing?'

Juba looked at the girls and felt a pang of guilt. 'I had a cloak—' he began, but Bouda interrupted him.

'Of course we haven't been questing,' she said. 'It's winter. Like soldiers, we've been training.'

Castor raised an eyebrow. 'Training?'

'Yes!' Bouda lifted her chin. 'Juba has been teaching some of us to read and write Latin. And to speak it, too. Properly, I mean. Like an orator.'

Castor raised both eyebrows. 'You?'

'Yes,' said Bouda. 'In this province women can be leaders. Also,' she continued, 'Juba and Ursula have been improving their Brittonic. They're almost fluent.'

Castor nodded ruefully. 'Your Brittonic is far better than mine.'

'Finally,' said Bouda. 'We have made a list of missing children and we will begin looking for them after the spring festival.'

'And where is this list?'

'In our heads,' said Bouda crisply, and began to recite. 'Bolianus, fifteen and of the Belgae, disappeared with his younger sister Bircha a week before Samhain. Dubonus, also fifteen, comes from a village near Isca Augusta. And the parents of thirteen-year-old Dirtha suspect Druids.'

Juba realised his mouth was hanging open so he closed it.

For a long moment Castor regarded each of them with his long-lashed grey eyes. 'So you *have* taken Flavia Gemina's challenge seriously?'

'As you have just heard,' said Juba, with a grateful look at Bouda.

Castor nodded. Then he tossed his hair out of his eyes. 'And how about your elder brother?' he said. 'Has Fronto been training, too?'

Chapter Twenty-Three
PAX ROMANA

It was nearly the end of April, and Fronto's basic training was almost completed.

As he dressed after a late afternoon session in the baths, he took a moment to admire his belly. Six months earlier it had been padded with a layer of blubber, now he was rock hard, the muscles clearly defined. His legs felt strong and solid. They could carry him twenty miles a day even with a sixty-pound load. He knew how to kill or disable a man with a pilum, gladius, pugio, lead sling-bullets and even his shield. He was also proficient at archery, and could hit a mark from thirty paces with his composite bow. Under Hamianus's tutoring he and the other seven in his contubernium had become so good with bow and arrows that they could hit the mark nine times out of ten.

Fronto liked sparring with men from different contubernia, using the heavy wooden swords, weighted with lead. He welcomed the ache of his muscles at night that meant he was getting stronger. He enjoyed regular visits to the opulent baths with his bunkmates.

But most of all he liked marching.

He liked the forward movement, feeling always in control, but also part of something bigger, with his friends around him.

He knew the chants by heart and could recite them without thinking. He no longer considered rain ominous. It was merely something to be accepted. He could march in wind and fog and even snow. He got to know the different sorts of trees and saw the first tiny sprouts of leaves appear. He saw birds building their nests. And the first lambs of spring. Sometimes on the march, he fell into a kind of trance. When he came back to the present, he found that his mind was clear and refreshed. He remembered lessons from his childhood, passages from epic poems he had memorised, things his father and mother had told him.

The only drawback to marching was that it made him hungry and sometimes there was no time to stop for food. Cicatrix had told them that chewing fennel seeds and adding a dash of vinegar to their water would stave off hunger pangs.

Because he did not like getting drunk, he did not go to the parts of the baths with beer, wine, girls and gambling. The fortress bath-house was massive and he found a quiet torchlit alcove in the hot room. There, wrapped in a towel and steaming gently, he would recite passages of Virgil's *Aeneid* to his bunkmates. Soon soldiers from other bunkhouses gathered after dinner to hear him recite. Some did not want to waste their money on girls and gambling. Some were Christians like Gelasinus. Others wanted to save their extra wages to give to their families or girlfriends. Soldiers could not officially marry, but three of the new recruits had families living in the town outside the walls.

The men loved Fronto's storytelling, and he had become one of the most popular soldiers in the fortress. Many gave him small gifts. They knew he loved honey cakes and he had a constant supply. Soon he did not have to pack fennel seeds for the march but could munch a honey cake while on the go.

Fronto's only worry was that so far he had never been in a

real battle. Would he be brave? Would he be able to kill a man?

'Why are you here?' asked Cicatrix on the first day of their last week. 'Why is the Roman army here in this fortress on the edges of the Empire?'

One of the recruits stepped forward. 'To kill barbarians, sir!' he said, and stepped smartly back.

'Incorrect!' blasted Cicatrix. 'Half of you ARE barbarians. Baby barbarians!'

The men laughed.

Fronto's heart was thudding but he took a step forward.

'Pax Romana, sir!' he said. 'We are here to keep the peace.' Then he stepped back.

'Correct!' blared Cicatrix. 'We are here as a peace-keeping force. To guard the borders of this province so that we can keep sending tin, wool and hunting dogs to Rome. Keeping the *Pax Romana* is the army's main objective.' He paused and then continued. 'Most of you might never see a real battle. You might spend your whole life collecting taxes, building roads and cleaning out aqueducts. You may ask why you have to drill with sword and shield? Why march for miles? Why learn to make a camp in an hour? Anyone?'

Dimpled Gelasinus stepped forward. 'Because one day we might have to march, make camp and fight, sir!' He stepped back into line.

'Correct!' shouted Cicatrix. 'Thankfully, most British tribes would rather squabble with each other than fight us. But one day they might unite.'

He looked around. 'Let's hope that day never comes. But if it does, then you will need all the skills you can muster. Also,' he added, 'not all of you will stay in this province forever. You may be transferred to a province whose natives are at war with

Rome. That is why you must master the skills of making camp, following orders and fighting. And that is why we drill. Drills give you skills!' Here he smacked his vine staff against the metal greave on his right leg. 'Drills are what prepare you for the unexpected. When you can follow orders in your sleep you are ready.'

He tucked his vine staff under his arm and strode along the rank of recruits.

'At the end of this week there will be a three-day exercise for those of you who want to join the Syrian Scorpions. It will be the hardest test you have faced.'

He stopped striding and turned to look at them.

'Those of you little girls who still want to join the cohort of Hamian archers, step forward!'

Fronto and Vindex exchanged glances and then nodded.

Vindex was the first to step forward.

And even though his knees were trembling, Fronto stepped forward, too.

Chapter Twenty-Four
VIOLARIA

More than anything, Ursula wanted to go with Castor. He was planning to leave the village the following day to find out more about the gathering of Druids, and also investigate a sighting of his brother near Glevum.

If she could ride out with him bearing her kitten on one shoulder and Loquax on the other, it would be her dream come true. They would find his brother and he would be happy again. Then the two of them could spend the rest of their lives riding all over Britannia and finding other lost children.

'Please take me with you?' she had begged him early that morning. She had been coming in from milking the goats, he going out with his hunting javelin.

Castor had given his head a sad shake. 'You're safer here in this village,' he said. 'Leave the questing to us men.'

'But Flavia Gemina was a Quester when she was young! And I'm as brave as any man!'

He only smiled and patted her head.

She had almost screamed in frustration as he strode off towards the woods.

Later, eating tasty flatbread whose flour she had ground,

kneaded and baked herself, she had an idea: she would ask the goddess for help.

'Will you come to help me pick flowers for Venus, Juba?'

'What?' He looked up from his scroll.

'It's almost Venus's special day: the Floralia!'

He gave her a crooked grin. 'I've got to prepare for my Latin class. Bring me back a garland of violets? I have a headache.'

'I think it's too early for violets,' she replied, 'but if I find any, I'll bring them.'

'I'll come with you,' said pretty Pacta.

'Me too!' said little Velvinna, who had just turned five.

'I'll come, too,' said Valatta. 'After all, it is a beautiful day.' Three other girls rose up, including Bouda.

Ursula took a basket from inside the door of the roundhouse and, with Meer on one shoulder and Loquax on the other, she led the others out into daylight.

It was a glorious morning with warm sunshine and sheep bleating. In the pen closest to the roundhouses were six new lambs, three of which she had watched being born.

Down the hill past the other pens and the newly planted barley field was one of the meadows where the sheep grazed. At the moment it was lushly green with scatterings of tiny daisies and islands of narcissi: tender trumpets of butter yellow surrounded by cream. It was bordered by the Green Woods, where the last snowdrops and the first bluebells dotted the shading verges.

The girls spread out to pick flowers.

Presently little Velvinna came up with a full basket. 'How do you make garlands?' she asked Ursula.

They sat on the grass and Ursula showed the little girl how to make a slit in the stem with her thumbnail and thread through other flowers. Other girls came over to sit in the warm sunshine. Pacta sang a song about spring flowers and Meer came down from her mistress's shoulder to explore.

Ursula finished first and placed a garland of yellow crocus, white snowdrops and purple bluebells on little Velvinna's head.

Her second garland clothed the little ivory Venus, so that she was no longer naked.

'Dear Venus,' Ursula breathed in the goddess's ear. 'I didn't drop you in the sacred spring because I believe you are a greater goddess than Sulis Minerva. You have answered so many of my prayers. Please may Castor take me with him to seek his brother.'

She held the statuette of Venus at arm's length and studied the ivory face above the pink and yellow blossoms. The goddess wore a faint smile.

'Look!' said Velvinna, placing a tiny garland on Meer's head. 'Meer has a garland!'

'Look!' said Valatta. 'Ursula has a garland.' She placed a garland on Ursula's head and Ursula laughed.

A little distance away Bouda held up her garland. 'How's this?' she called.

'It needs more narcissi,' said Ursula.

'Who are you going to give it to?' asked Valatta.

Bouda tipped her head and pretended to think. 'I might give it to a very special boy,' she said and shot Ursula a green glance. In the bright sunshine, her plaited hair flamed like molten bronze. Ursula felt a stab of jealousy. She knew Bouda was talking about Castor. Who else?

The sudden drumming of hoofbeats made them look to the Green Woods.

Two chariots had emerged from the trees and were bouncing towards them across the meadow. Both were low and light,

117

made of painted, springy wood. Both were driven by men in white hooded cloaks.

'Look! Chariots!' cried Ursula and clapped her hands in delight. She jumped up, eager to get a better look at the ponies pulling them: one pair was white and the other black.

'*Meeer!*' said Meer and scampered up to her left shoulder.

'*Druids in the Deathwoods!*' exclaimed Loquax, as he settled on her right hand shoulder.

Valatta gasped.

The hood of the white team's charioteer had just blown back to show a terrifying face. The driver was an old man with long white hair, black eyebrows and a blue-dyed beard in three plaits.

'It's the Druid!' Valatta clutched Ursula's arm so hard that it hurt. 'The Druid your brother saw in the Deathwoods!'

The girls watched in horror as the white-haired man steered his chariot towards Bouda, who must not have heard them coming out of the woods. She had bent to pick a violet and was only now looking round.

What happened next was both fast and slow. One moment Bouda was standing on the grassy meadow and the next she was in the chariot. As it wheeled they saw her face, wide-eyed and white as milk. The terrifying Druid gripped her upper arm in one hand and held a horsewhip in the other.

Ursula realised the reins must be tied around his waist, like a charioteer in Rome's Circus Maximus. Even as she watched, Bouda's abductor whipped his team of white ponies back up the meadow.

The Green Woods seemed to swallow them in one gulp.

Valatta and the other girls were screaming and running for the village, but Ursula saw something lying on the ground and ran to get it.

It was the beautiful garland that Bouda had been plaiting.

'*Meeer!*' cried Meer, clinging so hard that Ursula could feel her kitten's needle-sharp claws through three layers of cloth.

'*Ave, Domitian!*' warned Loquax, flapping above her head.

She heard the drumming of hoofbeats coming up behind.

Ursula whirled, and then froze.

The chariot pulled by black ponies was heading straight for her!

Chapter Twenty-Five
CORNICEN

Fronto was usually up a few moments before the cornicen blew his first blast, but one day near the end of April he was still in bed when it came.

The recruits had been told to prepare for two enforced marches of twenty miles per day in full kit followed by the ultimate test of character for those who wanted to join the Syrian Scorpions. Nobody could say what this test would be as it was the first time the fortress had hosted auxiliary troops. They only knew that it would be hard.

For the march, they would wear all their armour including their covered shields and they would carry the rest of their kit on wooden yokes resting over their shoulders. The kit included a spade and wooden spikes, for they would also have to make their own camp at the end of each march.

That was tomorrow. Meanwhile, they had one final day in the drill ground.

The bronze bleat of the trumpet brought Fronto out of bed in one movement. The others were rising, too: some quickly, some slowly, according to their temperament.

Beneath the colonnaded porch outside the front door, the barracks slave-boy Thuttenus was already stirring porridge over the brazier. He always put in a lot of salt but that didn't bother Fronto; he liked salt.

They ate out of their own bowls with their own spoons, some hunkered down on three-legged stools, others leaning against the wall or columns. Varro, who had a sweet tooth, spooned honey on his from his private store. Toothless Socrates added beer to his porridge and drank it down like thick soup.

Men from the other contubernia stood in little clumps outside their barracks in the shelter of the colonnade that ran along its front. Most were also eating porridge but a few munched sausages bought in town. Their breath came in white puffs but the cold air helped waken them.

Sometimes a man from one group would say something to a man in another, but mostly this was a time for them to ask how the others in their own contubernium had slept.

'What was wrong with you last night?' Socrates asked Fronto. 'You were turning like a pig on a spit. Worried about tomorrow's exercise?'

'I think I had bad dreams,' Fronto confessed. 'But I can't remember them.'

They all made the sign against evil.

A few of them had finished their porridge and were mopping their bowls with flat bread. No need to wash or scrub if you pressed hard with the bread and got all the stuff sticking to the inside of the bowl. One by one they put away their mess kits and headed off to the communal latrines.

There was often a queue outside the toilets at this time in the morning, for although there were several large multi-seaters positioned around the fortress, this was a popular time to go.

Back in Rome, Fronto had been used to sitting in a private space beneath the stairs. There he used old scraps of papyrus from his father's wastebasket to wipe his bottom: an almost unheard of luxury. Here, he had to share a sponge stick like everybody else, or use some leaves or moss.

After the initial shock of doing his business with fifty other men, Fronto had got used to it. Everybody except the legate and officers did it this way, and you could chat and gossip with your neighbours as they came and went.

It was while he was sitting on the communal toilet that Fronto first heard about Ursula and Bouda.

'Fronto!' cried Vindex from the doorway. 'Come quickly! Your sister has been captured by Druids.'

'What?' he cried over the babble of chattering men; he did not understand what Vindex was saying.

'Your brother and a friend of his are waiting outside the main gate. Hurry or we'll miss drills.'

Fronto gave himself a final wipe and put the sponge-stick in the bucket for the next person to use.

Outside it was chilly and overcast, with oppressive grey clouds.

Fronto hurried with Vindex to the Porta Praetoria, the gate he had entered that first evening nearly half a year before.

'Outside,' Vindex pointed. 'They're waiting just outside.'

Fronto gave him a nod of thanks and went through the gate, tapping *right, left, right*. He was not wearing his cloak, helmet or weapons, just his tunics, leggings and chain mail vest. And a felt skullcap on his head.

Two figures stood with their backs to him, looking at the stalls and taverns at the water's edge. They both wore hooded cloaks: one dark grey and the other a dark brown that he recognised as his own cloak, the one he had given to his brother.

'Juba!' he said, and then, 'Castor?' as they both turned.

122

'Fronto!' cried Juba. He stepped forward as if to embrace his brother, but then hesitated. 'You look so different. You look like a soldier.'

'I am a soldier,' said Fronto. 'My basic training finishes at the end of this week. Then I hope to join a cohort of Syrian archers.' Fronto turned to Castor. 'How are you?'

'No time for that,' said Juba, and took a step closer. 'Ursula and Bouda have been abducted.'

'What?'

'They were picking flowers in the meadow,' said Juba, 'when two chariots came out of the woods. The girls said the one who took Bouda had white hair and blue plaits for his beard.'

Fronto stared. 'The face I saw in the Deathwoods!'

Juba nodded. 'Yes. Everyone is sorry they didn't believe you.'

Castor said, 'There have been rumours of a Druid uprising.'

Fronto frowned. 'Traditionally, Druids don't rise up,' he said. 'They incite others to rise up and curse the enemy.'

Castor rolled his eyes. 'All right, then: a Druid-led uprising.'

'Where?'

'At a place near Lactodurum, a hundred miles away.'

'It takes six days to march there,' said Fronto. 'I know because we've done it.' Then he looked at his brother. 'You think Druids took the girls? But why?'

'We don't know,' said Juba. 'But we're going up there to look for them now.'

The sudden blare of a trumpet made Fronto start. He turned to look behind him. Vindex stood just inside the gate, waiting.

'Why did you come to me?' said Fronto. 'If I leave the fortress they'll execute me for desertion.'

'We thought you could muster a scouting party,' said Juba, 'and help us search for them.'

123

'How could I muster a scouting party? I'm still a recruit; the lowest of the low!'

'Talk to your superior,' said Castor. 'Tell him about the sighting of Druids. Maybe he'll let you go and investigate.'

For the first time in months, Fronto's thoughts were frozen. He gave his head a small shake to clear it. 'All right, I'll ask someone. Can you meet me back here an hour before dusk?' He pointed. 'Meet me at The Legionary's Rest Tavern when you hear the trumpet for dinner,' he said. 'They make good sausages.'

The trumpet blared again and Fronto turned to go. Juba caught his arm and held him.

'Fronto, we *can't* wait until this evening. Every moment counts. You have to come now or not at all. Ask your commander if you can get a few days' leave.'

Fronto's heart was beating hard and he tasted panic.

'I'm sorry, Juba,' he said. 'If I miss today's drill then I'll miss my chance to join the Syrian archers. I might even have to do my basic training all over again. And if I come without asking permission,' he added, 'then my own bunkmates will beat me to death for deserting! Goodbye and good luck! I hope you find the girls.'

Chapter Twenty-Six
VITIS

Fronto tried to concentrate on drills, but the thought of Ursula and Bouda abducted by Druids haunted him.

By noon he could bear it no longer. At the midday break in training, Fronto approached Cicatrix with dry mouth and beating heart. 'Permission to speak, sir?'

The centurion looked up from the bench with a scowl. 'What is it, Fronto? I'm in a bad mood. I hope it's not some feeble excuse for why you were late this morning.'

'It was my brother at the gate, sir,' stammered Fronto. 'He thinks that Druids might have kidnapped my sister and my um . . . girlfriend.'

'Get out of here!' Cicatrix stood up and raised his vine staff threateningly. 'If there's one thing I hate, it's a soldier who shirks his duty and then makes excuses. And that is the most ridiculous excuse I have ever heard.'

Fronto took a breath. 'But, sir, he says there might be a Druid-led uprising and—'

Thwack! The staff struck Fronto's helmet so violently that he fell against one of the columns.

His ears were ringing but he still heard the centurion's angry words: 'You've only got a few days left of basic training. One more peep and I'll start you at the beginning with the next lot of recruits!'

Fronto pushed himself away from the column and stumbled back to where his friends were waiting.

Vindex looked at him in alarm. 'You're bleeding!'

Fronto took off his helmet and Vindex said, 'It's your ear. Your skullcap wasn't over that bit and a rivet must have cut you. It will heal,' he added.

But Fronto's head throbbed for the rest of the day and most of the night.

The throb was a dull ache when they set out on their first long march early the next morning.

Dawn was red – a bad omen – and they marched double pace almost all day, with only four short breaks.

Finally, when the sun was setting behind leaden clouds, they stopped to make camp.

After a false spring, a cold snap had brought plunging temperatures. Freezing rain turned to sleet as they began to dig their portion of ditch. Each man hammered his own stakes into the ditch. Only then did they pitch their four goat-leather tents, hurrying to get them up before the light failed. Gelasinus hurt his hand while putting in his stakes so Fronto and Vindex helped him, but this set them all back. It was hard putting up tents in freezing sleet with only sputtering torches to give light.

Fronto had heard of people being too tired to eat. He had never believed such a thing could happen to him. But that night when he rolled up in his beaver-skin cloak he plunged into a sort of unconsciousness.

It seemed only a moment later that a hand was shaking him awake. 'Get up, or you'll be left behind!' said Vindex.

'Is it night?'

'No, it's dawn.' Fronto felt a copper beaker of hot-spiced wine being thrust into his hands and he drank it gratefully.

And so they started the forty-mile march back to Isca. But driving sleet meant they would not reach the fortress by nightfall. And so they had to pitch camp again, digging the trench, hammering in the wooden palisade spikes and putting up the slippery leather tents in freezing rain with fingers so numb they could barely feel them.

The enemy struck shortly before dawn.

Fronto and Vindex were on the graveyard watch, as punishment for being late to drill three days before.

If he had been well-rested, and if his muscles had not been screaming with pain, Fronto might have had the wits to fight back when a figure emerged from the sleet, brought the back of Fronto's cloak over his head and bound his arms to his sides. Bound, blinded and half-deafened by his beaver-skin cloak, he thought he heard a muffled protest behind him. They must have grabbed Vindex, too.

Now he was being prodded out of the camp and down a slippery hill. Once he almost slipped but managed to right himself at the last moment. He heard Vindex gasp and a moment later he did, too, as his feet splashed through the icy water of a small stream. Then up another slippery bank, through brambles that tore at his tunic and braccae. He stumbled blindly across an uneven field with long wet grass and a scent of cowpats. Finally he was shoved up four wooden stairs into an echoing box of wood.

Something about the feel of his hobnails on the wooden floor reminded him of somewhere familiar. But before his exhausted mind could identify it, his fur cloak was whipped away and the cold struck him like a bucket of water. He was in a room like a big wooden box, dimly lit by a birch-bark torch.

Out of the flickering shadows loomed a hooded face, ghastly white and with painted spirals of brown.

'Who are you?' The barbarian held a torch and spoke Latin in a heavily accented, garlic-stinking voice.

Fronto had been trained to give only his name and legion.

'I . . . My name is Julius Mensa,' he stammered. 'A recruit with the Second Augusta.'

'Tell us password for today,' said another accented voice behind him. 'The password of the great fortress.'

Fronto started to turn his head to see who was speaking when the first man gave him an open-handed slap on his cheek. 'Don't look! Just speak. Tell us password!'

Fronto had never been slapped in his life. He was more shocked by the stinging intimacy of flesh on flesh than he had been by any of the blows from Cicatrix's twisted vine staff.

He gaped at the man.

'Tell us!' His interrogator slapped his other cheek.

Fear and exhaustion churned in Fronto's belly and for a moment he thought he might vomit. Then he took a deep breath. 'My name is Julius Mensa,' he repeated. 'I'm doing my basic training with the Second Augusta.'

Behind him in the shadows, Vindex was whimpering.

'I will ask you one more time,' said the man. 'What is password?'

Fronto's mind was frozen. He could not think. He could only whisper over and over, 'Jupiter, help us. Jupiter, help us.'

'Maybe your friend will be helping us,' said the unseen man.

Fronto heard Vindex yelp. They must be torturing him.

'What is password?' the man behind him asked Vindex.

'I don't know! I don't know!' cried his friend.

'We've killed all the others in your tent and we'll kill you, too,' said the first man. 'Tell us password of great fortress of Isca Augusta.'

Fronto shook his head but behind him Vindex sobbed, 'All right! I'll tell!'

'No!' cried Fronto, turning his head. 'Don't tell them! Thousands of men's lives might depend on us keeping quiet.'

A knee in his stomach brought him gasping onto the raw plank floor. Someone kicked him in the ribs and he felt his chain armour dig in.

'Tell us,' came a voice through a ringing in his ears.

'No,' came Vindex's voice. 'I won't tell you the password. My name is Lucius Vindex of the Second Augusta.'

Fronto heard the two men confer in a strange, guttural language. Then the flickering light returned to Fronto and he looked up to see one hooded man holding the torch and another with a pair of iron shears, just like the ones Tonsor used to trim their hair in the bath house.

'I am going to cut off your friend's fingers, one by one,' said the man with the shears to Fronto. 'Unless you talk.'

Fronto closed his eyes. 'Jupiter help us, Jupiter help us!' he muttered. But Jupiter did not come to his aid and he could not bear to see or even hear his friend being tortured.

'All right!' he gasped. 'All right! I'll tell you what you want to know.'

Chapter Twenty-Seven
TESSERA

Fronto was about to tell his torturers the password, when he realised something didn't make sense. He opened his eyes.

'Who are you?' he asked, his heart pounding in his throat. 'You're not Britons. I know their language and it's nothing like what you were speaking.'

'We'll ask the questions,' said Shears Barbarian, but instead of cutting off one of Vindex's fingers he took a step back. As he did so, flickering torchlight illuminated his shoes.

Another revelation sparked in Fronto's mind and created a flame of hope.

'You're both wearing caligae.' He pointed with a trembling finger. 'Those are regulation army boots.'

'Maybe we got them off dead Romans,' said Shears Barbarian.

'Or maybe we had them made by a cobbler in our barbarian village,' said Torch Barbarian.

'No,' said Fronto. 'I can tell those come from Brutus's workshop in the fortress. He does that twist with the straps. And your socks are like the ones they sell in the armoury, too.'

'Observant under extreme pressure,' said Torch Barbarian in Latin to the man with the shears.

'Yes,' said the other. They looked at each other, nodded and pulled their hoods back.

'We're not Britons,' said the man with the shears. 'We're from the first Hamian cohort: the Syrian Scorpions. This was a little test to see how you would react under pressure.'

'What?' Fronto stared stupidly. The men both had curly dark hair, cut short in army regulation. Now that their hoods were back, he could see their faces weren't pale with brown clay markings, but the opposite. The brown spirals were made by a finger wiping off pale clay to show the skin colour *underneath*. He should have noticed that, too.

Beside him, Vindex started sobbing.

'Give them their cloaks,' said Torch to Shears. 'You were very observant to notice my shoes,' he told Fronto. 'Can you tell us anything else about who we are or where we are?'

Fronto looked around at the bare wooden room. 'We're in an empty granary,' he stammered. 'A storeroom for grain and other foodstuffs.'

'Good. What else?'

'I don't know what else,' he said, close to tears.

'All right then,' said the Syrian in his distinctive accent. 'What's your name again?'

Fronto told him. A third man appeared in the doorway. 'Done?' he asked.

'Yes,' said Torch Syrian. 'You can take these two back to fortress.'

Clutching their cloaks around them, Fronto and Vindex stumbled down the stairs after the third man, who also had a torch. It had finally stopped raining and the clouds had fled. Faint starlight showed the looming black wall of the fortress. They were at the northeast gate: so close!

All this time they had been within shouting distance of the fortress.

'Back to your bunks,' said the Syrian. 'Your centurion and optio will tell you what to do.'

The guard at the gate waved them through. The fortress looked strange: dark and silent, with only a few torches burning and the crunch of sentries' footfalls on the walkways above. When they got back to their bunkhouse, they found it deserted. 'Where are the others?' Fronto asked Vindex.

'Probably still asleep in their tents,' said Vindex miserably.

Fronto did not reply.

He ought to have been relieved, but the memory of his cowardice tormented him. He had been so close to giving the password. Another moment and he would have spilled it out. How could he ever hope to be a soldier?

In his mind, he relived the moment in the Deathwoods when he had seen the face with spiky hair and snakes for a beard. He saw himself throw down his bow and stumble through the black oaks, falling off the log and into the brook, rising up wet and shaking to hear mocking laughter.

He could still see Bouda's look of scorn. Bouda, whose copper hair and green eyes made his heart beat fast. Bouda, whose life was now in danger and whom he had refused to help rescue.

He realised that he would always be a coward. Even six months with the army had not helped.

His churning stomach drove him out of his bunk to the nearest latrines, but he was sick on the way. Afterwards, gulping the cold night air he dug his fingernails into his palms.

He wished he had never been born.

He understood why warriors in the *Iliad* and the *Aeneid* preferred death to dishonour.

And he realised that if he too was prepared to die, there was a way he could make up for his cowardice.

He would leave the army to save Ursula and Bouda.

And if they captured him and beat him to death for desertion, so be it.

Because now Fronto knew that death was preferable to a cowardly life.

III

Chapter Twenty-Eight
DEFECTIO

Desertion proved surprisingly easy, thanks to a thick spring fog and his beaver-skin cloak.

'I dropped my coin pouch somewhere between here and our camp,' he told the sentry. It was Postumus, the guard nicknamed 'Cerberus' who had once refused them entry. But on this occasion he was distracted by two sobbing recruits coming into the fort and he waved Fronto through without looking. Unlike Hades, it wasn't hard to get out; it was hard to get back in.

Fronto walked north along the road until the fog swallowed the fortress behind him. Without his armour, helmet and furca – the soldier's yoke from which he hung his gear – he could pass for an ordinary traveller on the road. Unless you noticed his caligae and the bulge of a quiver under his cloak and part of the composite bow peeking out beneath its hem.

As he walked, he talked to himself.

'How could you turn Juba away like that?' he asked himself. 'Ursula is your sister! You are paterfamilias now and you've been doing a terrible job of it. But you'll do better now, won't you? Even if it kills you.'

To take his mind off these thoughts he tried to remember what Juba had told him. Druids had abducted the girls and there had been rumours of a gathering near Lactodurum, an easy six days' march from Isca. He had just done two forced marches of forty miles. If he pushed himself to the limit, he might be able to do it in three days.

He had all the money he owned in a pouch around his neck. Down the back of his tunic was his statuette of Jupiter, wrapped in a clean napkin. His army belt already contained useful things, including his tinder-pouch with its essential iron, flint, and some horse-hoof fungus.

His small, flat-bottomed cooking pan was down the front of his tunic and his water skin was full. When he had first carried all these things, along with the pack attached to his furca, they had made his muscles ache. Now he hardly felt them.

At around noon he stopped and gnawed on some hard tack and took some swigs of posca from his waterskin. The steady forward movement of walking had lifted his spirits and given him hope.

He could smell spring in the air. That gave him hope, too.

Strangely, the thing that gave him the most courage was knowing that there were worse things than death.

Even so, when he heard the hoofbeats of horses coming up the road from the south, he vaulted the roadside ditch and hid in the bushes.

Chapter Twenty-Nine
SOCII

Fronto parted the bushes as the riders appeared, shapes in the mist. Were there two? Or three? As they came closer he could make out two men on horseback leading a third riderless mount. One was a bull-necked man and the other a youth.

Vindex!

The youth was his friend Vindex and the other was . . .

Fronto squinted and then his eyes widened. The other man was Cicatrix, dressed as a civilian.

Without his helmet the centurion looked very different, but there was no mistaking the hideous face with its massive chin and worm-like scar.

Had Vindex betrayed him? Had he brought Cicatrix on the route he knew Fronto must take?

Impossible. Vindex was his friend; the first real friend he had ever had.

It was more likely that Cicatrix blamed Vindex and was going to punish him if they couldn't find Fronto.

He couldn't let that happen, even if it meant suffering the punishment of a deserter. Taking a breath, he pushed out of the bushes and ran forward. 'Don't blame Vindex!' Fronto shouted. 'He didn't know anything about it!'

Cicatrix's mount reared up in alarm.

The centurion cursed as he tried to regain control of his horse.

'Fronto!' exclaimed Vindex, dismounting and embracing his friend. 'Thank the gods we found you! What were you thinking? You know desertion is punishable by death.'

'I know. But I had to do something.' He glared defiantly up at the centurion. 'Don't blame Vindex,' he said again. 'It was my decision to leave.'

Cicatrix swung down off his horse.

'Don't worry,' came the gruff reply, 'he's not in trouble. Neither are you.'

'I'm not?'

Cicatrix shook his head. 'We don't tell the recruits,' he said, 'but we usually give you a little slack. If you've had enough of army life then just pay back any money you were advanced and leave your armour.'

'I didn't *want* to leave, sir. I left because I wanted to help my sister. And also to recover my honour.'

Cicatrix's ugly face twisted into a frown. 'What do you mean: *recover your honour?*'

Fronto stared at the ground. 'When the Syrians took us and threatened to torture us, I was afraid. I almost gave away the password.'

Cicatrix gave a bark of laughter. 'Son, you and your friend here were the only ones who *didn't* give up the password.'

Fronto looked up in surprise. 'We were?'

Cicatrix shrugged. 'It's almost impossible not to break under such pressure when you're cold, exhausted and frightened. Especially if it's the first time you've gone through such an ordeal. The exercise is designed to prepare you for situations that might occur. And to show you how easy it is to give in to fear. So don't be ashamed.'

Fronto swallowed and looked down at the road again. In his mind's eye, he could still see the look of scorn on Bouda's pretty face.

'But how can I learn to be brave?'

He flinched as Cicatrix grasped his shoulders, but the centurion's hands were firm and warm.

'Son, have you ever heard people say that real courage is feeling the fear but doing it anyway?'

'You've said that many times.'

'And it's true. But sometimes it's also foolish to feel the fear and do it anyway.'

Fronto looked up, puzzled. 'What do you mean, sir?'

'Fear can be our friend. It warns us when danger is near.'

'So we should just run away?'

Cicatrix let go of Fronto and gave his head a small shake. 'Let me put it this way. Say a legion is on the move and scouts report that the enemy is lying in wait. The legion would be foolish to march into a trap, correct?'

'Yes.'

'Well, think of fear as that scout. Its job is to warn us. Then it's up to the commander to decide whether to go forward, back or round. The problem,' he continued, 'is when fear becomes our commander, not our advisor. We need to make something else our commander.'

'What?'

'You tell me.'

'Honour?'

'Yes, but also common sense. We are not dumb beasts.

You need to put your mind in control, not your gut. Do you understand?'

'I think so,' said Fronto.

'Do you want another chance to prove you have courage?'

Fronto nodded. 'More than anything in the world. But my sister . . .'

'I know. You said. And I should have listened to you. But my leg was aching and I was in a bad mood.' He shook his head. 'Yesterday, while you were on your exercise, the legate called us all to his quarters. He had also heard rumours of a Druid-led uprising and warned us to be on the alert. That is why he gave permission for me to take two men on a scouting mission.'

Fronto's heart leapt and he looked up eagerly. 'You mean I can still look for Ursula and Bouda? And you'll both come with me?'

Cicatrix chuckled. 'Why else do you think we're dressed like a couple of Batavian sausage-sellers? Have a look in your saddle packs,' he added. 'It's something from the Syrian Scorpions.'

Fronto went to the riderless horse and opened one of the leather saddle packs.

'Lorica squamata,' he said. 'Fish-scale armour!'

'There's a helmet in the other one,' said Vindex.

Cicatrix gave his gap-toothed grin. 'The Syrians say if you come back you're their first choice.'

'I'm in, too!' Vindex's eyes were shining. 'Only they didn't give me the armour.'

Fronto swallowed hard and looked at his friend. Suddenly his vision was blurry and he had to blink away tears.

'Oh, don't be little girls about it!' groaned Cicatrix. 'Get on your horse and ride. We don't have a moment to lose.'

Chapter Thirty
TINTINNABULA

The tinkle of bronze wind chimes and the cooing of a wood pigeon brought Ursula gently awake.

She had been dreaming of the moment the white-cloaked youth had pulled her up into his chariot.

The moment she saw his smooth-cheeked face she had relaxed and laughed.

'Aren't you afraid?' he asked her.

'Of course not! I'm happy that you're taking me with you.'

Then he had shown his white teeth in a laugh and told her to hold on tight.

It was only when she had looked more closely at his handsome face that she finally understood who he really was.

Excitement filled her as she gripped the bent wood of the chariot frame and breathlessly watched the trunks of the trees blur past. The webbed leather floor of the chariot was springy beneath her feet and sometimes she bounced so high that she almost felt airborne. She remembered how the smell of the horses and the urgent drumming of their hooves had filled her head.

Meer had clung to her shoulder while Loquax flapped overhead and she had laughed every time she looked at her smiling abductor.

He told her to call him Raven.

After they emerged from the woods and turned onto the road to Aquae Sulis they settled down to a steady but brisk trot.

'Where are you taking me?' she asked him.

'To a wonderful secret place.'

'Will Bouda be there, too?'

'She will be nearby.'

'My brother and the villagers will worry about us,' she said.

'Don't worry,' he said, 'all will be explained.'

He took a suck from a goatskin flask and handed it to her. She had expected water or posca and was surprised to taste something like sweet liquid bread, but with a sharp green aftertaste.

'What is it?'

'I call it green beer. It helps you not to be afraid.'

'I'm not afraid. Venus has answered my prayer.'

She had another long drink of the green beer and laughed to see woods, wagons and pilgrims float past. The steady clop of the ponies' hooves made a rhythmic chant in her head and soon they were past Aquae Sulis and heading north on a new road.

It took them three days to reach their destination and the journey seemed like a dream. Raven taught her to drive a chariot sitting or standing. He told her the names of all the trees and shrubs, and how each was special. Bread, cheese and goatsmilk served as meals and at night they found stables and slept in sweet-smelling hay near the ponies.

Whenever Ursula asked about Bouda, Raven told her that his father was a wise magician who had great things planned for them both, but that Bouda was being taken to a different place.

They arrived at dusk on the third day. The ponies turned off the road and went down a darkening tunnel of trees to a clearing lit by a few smoking torches.

144

Ursula was shivering, from excitement and exhaustion. She dimly remembered a girl of about fourteen with silver-blonde hair. The girl helped her down from the chariot and led her into a small roundhouse and gave her strange-tasting soup. Another girl with curly brown hair fussed over Meer and found a bowl of milk. Loquax fluttered up to the top of a loom and put himself to bed.

Now, on the fourth morning, she woke to the sound of wind chimes and pigeons, and sunshine streaming through the single open door of the small roundhouse.

Her first thought was to see Raven again.

She sat up, stretched and looked around. The roundhouse was deserted and neither Meer nor Loquax were anywhere to be seen. Heart beating, Ursula swung her legs off the bed shelf. Dizzy with hunger, she found her boots, slipped them on and stood up.

Brilliant sunlight poured through the single door and drew her forward.

She stopped at the threshold, enchanted by the sight of a village unlike any she had seen in Italia or Britannia.

The settlement consisted of three tents, two huts and a roundhouse: each one different from the next. A round tent of red-dyed goatskin with a door flap of green and blue was pitched next to a chicken coop topped with a tiny thatched roof. One hut was half buried in the side of a hill. As Ursula moved out into the bright morning sunshine, she saw an ancient oak tree at the centre of the dwellings. A hundred fluttering ribbons hung from its branches among the balls of mistletoe. Wind chimes made of bronze hung from some of its lower branches, making the tinkly sound she had heard earlier.

Beneath the oak five young people sat cross-legged around a

small bronze cauldron. Their backs were straight and their eyes were closed. The three boys were wearing the most extraordinary clothes Ursula had ever seen: striped tunics that ended in short leggings instead of a skirt. The girls wore dresses of the same silky fabric, which Ursula knew was woven from sweet nettles.

'*Meeer!*' said Meer, rising up from the lap of one of the girls. The kitten ran to Ursula, leapt onto her cloak and scampered up to her left shoulder.

The five of them opened their eyes and laughed when Loquax flew down from the oak and lighted on her right shoulder with a cheerful '*Carpe diem!*'

'She's awake!' said a girl with a cloud of brown curls.

'Good morning, Ursula,' said a boy with reddish brown hair. 'We hope you feel better.'

'Good morning, Ursula!' said the others. They were all smiling at her with strangely bright eyes.

The silver-blonde girl stood up in a graceful, fluid movement. 'Are you feeling better?'

Ursula nodded and looked around at them. 'Who are you?' she asked. 'And why did Raven bring me here?'

'Our leader brought you because you're special,' said the silver-blonde. 'Bards sing of the girl with kitten and bird. Even our leader has heard of you.'

'This is a kind of school,' said the red-haired boy.

'Is your leader called Raven?' Ursula looked around for the boy who had taken her.

The girl with the silver hair laughed. 'No. Raven Wing is our leader's son. My name is Bircha, but you can call me Nimble Tree.'

'I'm her brother,' said a boy with a strong nose and light brown hair. 'They call me Standing Hawk.'

146

'I'm Dirtha,' said the girl with curly brown hair. 'They call me Dancing Wren.'

'I'm One Ember,' said the youth with red-brown hair. 'And that is Sneezing Vole.'

Ursula gasped. 'You're the missing children.' She pointed at curly-haired Dirtha. 'You were abducted by Druids!'

The girl laughed. 'We weren't really abducted. We were chosen, like you. We *want* to be Druids.'

One Ember spread his arms. 'Welcome to Mistletoe Oak,' he said, 'our Druid School.'

Chapter Thirty-One
VISCUM ALBUM

Ursula looked around at the smiling boys and girls of Mistletoe Oak. 'Don't you want to go home?' she asked them. 'Don't you miss your parents?'

They all smiled and shook their heads. 'We love it here,' said blonde Nimble Tree. 'We have hardly any chores and we're learning to understand the trees and animals.'

'We're memorising the sacred teachings,' added the boy with dark curly hair and pale eyes called Sneezing Vole.

'There are seven levels,' said Dirtha, and she recited, 'Leaf, Fur, Feather, Cloud, Star, Fire and Word. We're on the first level where we learn to hear the trees and shrubs.'

'Really?' Ursula's heart skipped a beat. 'Can you really hear what plants are saying?'

'If you have the gift,' said Standing Hawk.

'And the potion,' added Nimble Tree.

'Can you teach me how to hear the trees? And animals? Can you give me some of the potion?'

They looked at each other, then the boy with reddish-brown hair nodded. 'Some of us are about to go into the sacred grove to finish making the wicker man. You can take some potion and by the time we get there it should have taken effect.'

The blonde girl looked into the cauldron. 'There's just enough left for one,' she said.

'Yes please!' cried Ursula. 'Also,' she added, 'do you have anything to eat? I'm ravenous.'

'We have food,' said the boy with curly black hair and pale eyes, 'but it's best to take the potion on an empty stomach. Which do you want? Food or potion?'

Ursula's stomach growled fiercely but she ignored it. 'Potion,' she replied without hesitation.

They all laughed and Nimble Tree dipped a horn beaker into the cauldron.

Ursula sat cross-legged like the others, took the beaker and drank it down in three gulps.

It tasted like mushrooms, with a bitter finish in her throat. She coughed and they patted her back.

When she had recovered her breath, she looked around hopefully. 'Where's Raven?' she asked.

'He went to see his father, our leader,' said Bircha. 'He'll be back soon. Then he'll join us in the woods. There's a special glade where the magic is even deeper than it is here.'

'I think I hear him now,' said Dirtha.

Ursula heard it, too: the soft clop of ponies' hooves, the creak of wood and leather, the jingle of bronze yoke rings.

She turned and waited for him to come into view. Had she been dreaming? Had she imagined him?

No, was the answer.

He drove the chariot to a yellow tent and jumped lightly down.

'Hello, Ursula,' he said with a heart-stopping smile. 'How are you this beautiful morning?'

'Ursula wants to hear the trees,' said the reddish-haired boy. 'She's taken some potion.'

Raven laughed. 'Wonderful. Do you want to help me brush down the ponies first?'

She could not reply. Was she dreaming? How had he brought her to this magical place where she would soon understand the speech of trees?

'Ursula?' he said. 'Are you all right?'

She nodded and followed him to the yellow tent. Inside she saw water troughs and food mangers on the straw-covered ground. And a pretty chestnut mare.

She clapped her hands in delight. 'This tent is a stable!' she cried.

Raven grinned and nodded.

Once the ponies were unhitched, they each grasped a handful of straw and began to groom the sturdy beasts. Ursula had so many questions but first she had to know if her theory about him was right.

'Raven?' she said, her heart beating hard.

'Yes?' He was brushing the pony's flank.

She took a deep breath. 'Where were you born?' she asked. 'And what is your real name?'

He flicked his hair out of his eyes. 'Why do you ask?' he said.

Ursula took another deep breath. 'Were you born in Ostia and do you have a long-lost identical twin brother named Castor?'

For a moment Raven stared at her. Then he burst out laughing.

Chapter Thirty-Two
QUERCUS

Juba swung off his pony with a grimace. He had been on horseback for three days: a long stretch from Isca to Glevum to Corinium, then forty miles east to a crossroads called 'Two Forts', and finally north towards Lactodurum.

Now it was mid-afternoon, and the muscles of his legs and lower back were aching. But he didn't want to let Castor see his weakness so he kept quiet. The older boy was crouched by a bush looking down through the leaves. Rumours passed on by an innkeeper had led them to this part of the ridge. And now Castor had found something.

Juba crouched down beside Castor and peered through a gap in the branches.

In a sunny glade below was a strange woodland settlement. At its centre was an oak tree that fluttered with coloured yarn and ribbons. There was a small wattle and daub roundhouse with a mushroom-shaped thatched roof like the houses at Soft Hill. But there were also three colourful tents and a house seemingly built into the grassy south-facing hillside.

Near the house built into the hill was a goat tied to a peg. A few hens scratched in sunny places and pigeons cooed.

'Look at that oak!' Juba said. 'This must be the camp. Caesar wrote that Druids worship the oak and use the mistletoe for magic potions.'

'Maybe,' said Castor. 'But I can't imagine more than fifteen or twenty people living there. Thirty at the most. Is that the Druid-led uprising?'

'We're in the right place,' said Juba. 'Two miles from Lactodurum near the site of Boudica's defeat . . .'

'But where is everyone?' murmured Castor, nibbling his thumbnail. 'There's nobody here but those chickens. And that goat.'

A breeze made the wind chimes tinkle and Juba saw long striped tunics flapping on a line behind one of the tents.

'Smoke,' whispered Juba, 'always betrays the presence of people. Look!' He pointed to the small roundhouse, where the faintest trace of smoke was beginning to drift up from the thatched roof. 'Someone must be here,' he whispered. 'They're stoking the hearth fire.'

'But look there!' Castor pointed to the northwest, where half a dozen threads of smoke were rising above the trees into the blue sky. 'That's more likely to be the site of a warrior camp! How far away do you think they are?'

'A mile,' said Juba. 'A mile and a half at most. And I count six fires. No, seven.'

Down in the strange village, the goat bleated as a figure emerged from the small roundhouse. It was a girl about Castor's age, perhaps a little older. She was tall and slender with straight silver-blonde hair and a blue and tan striped tunic. She wore a plaited blue ribbon around her forehead and hair.

'She's beautiful,' breathed Juba.

'She may be beautiful,' whispered Castor drily, 'but I don't think she's a Druid. According to all the sources they are bearded old men in white robes, carrying golden sickles with which they will peel the skin from your body.'

Juba nodded ruefully. 'Unless they decide to burn you alive.'

'Or rip your still-beating heart from your chest,' said Castor.

'So what's it to be?' Juba said. 'Stay here and spy on the beautiful girl or try to find the Druid camp?'

Castor raised an eyebrow and Juba nearly burst out laughing. He was almost beginning to like him.

Chapter Thirty-Three
POTIO

The mushroom-tasting potion had made Ursula dizzy and her mouth dry, but at least it took away her hunger.

By the time they reached the grove, the leaves of the trees had started to glow.

Her six new friends were making a wicker man like the one the villagers had burned at Soft Hill half a year before. The two girls were sitting cross-legged working on the head while the boys built up the torso.

Ursula helped the girls until the light in the trees and shrubs started to pulse. Then she stopped to stare.

By the time the boys were fixing the head on the wicker man, she had begun to see pictures in the branches of the trees. Not coloured pictures like frescos on a wall, but outlined shapes, like the figures scratched into the black glaze of an antique Greek vase her father once owned.

'Do things look different?' asked Raven, jumping down from the torso of the wicker man. Above him, Sneezing Vole and Standing Hawk were using vines to attach the head to the neck.

Ursula nodded. She was staring at four trees with tender leaves just beginning to show. 'The leaves of the trees are tiny green lamps, and I see soldiers marching forward in the branches.'

'Do you think she has the gift?' she heard Hawk whisper to Vole.

Ursula looked up. 'A wise old lady told me I have the gift of Fur and Feathers,' she said. The potion had made her hearing much sharper. But she didn't wait for a reply. Now she could hear something else.

'I can hear whispering,' she said. 'Or maybe it's just the wind in the leaves.'

'Go closer,' said Raven. 'Choose one of the trees and go closer.'

Ursula looked around at the glowing grove. Some instinct drew her to a slender tree with mostly white bark. 'What tree is this?' she asked Raven.

'We call it silver birch. Close your eyes,' he added. 'Sometimes things you see can distract you from the unseen.'

Ursula pressed her hands against the bark and closed her eyes. The trunk tingled against her palms and she felt a strange emotion flow from the tree into her heart. 'Oh!' she cried. 'She's alive. The tree is alive.'

'Of course it's alive,' said Raven. 'It's a tree.'

'No, but it's more than that. She knows I'm here. She knows it's me.' She took her hands away, overwhelmed by the knowledge.

'Listen carefully,' said Raven. 'Can you hear what they're saying?'

Ursula closed her eyes again and breathed slowly. The leaves were whispering.

Be still and listen, the Birch seemed to say. Her voice was like her trunk, slender and silvery. *You have been given a great gift. The gift to understand us and know that we understand you.*

You are called, whispered an Oak, his voice both deep and textured.

You can be anything. Go anywhere, whispered an Ash. Her voice was green and soft, like a breeze on a late summer evening.

But first you must learn to listen, said the Birch.

Ursula hugged the tree. *Yes,* she whispered in Brittonic. *I am here. I am listening.*

She wondered if she were imagining this: making it up in her head.

But she knew it was real. Although their voices sounded like nothing more than wind rustling leaves, she could feel them as a vibration against the cheekbone she had laid against the trunk. It was as if Meer was purring there, and not on her shoulder.

She had an idea. Could she speak to Meer?

Eyes still closed, she pushed away from the tree.

'Meer,' she whispered. 'Can you speak to me, too?'

Meer's purr grew louder and Ursula felt the tiny pinprick of claws as Meer kneaded her left shoulder by the base of her neck. *I love you,* Meer seemed to be saying. *And I am happy to be your kitten.*

'Can you understand the trees?' Raven's voice sounded strange after the trees' whispers.

'Yes,' she said. 'And my kitten, too.'

'Be careful. Don't run before you can walk.'

Ursula nodded and turned her attention back to the rustling voices.

Don't ignore us, the trees were saying. *Don't forget that we are aware of you. Our roots go down deep. We feel your footfalls, your hoofbeats, your wagon wheels. We sense your life force. Be still. Know that we are here.*

Little Bear, whispered the Birch.

Little Bear, purred the Oak.

Little Bear, murmured the Ash.

Ursula gasped. 'They know my name!' she whispered. 'They're calling me Little Bear!'

'Good!' said Raven, and even with her eyes closed she knew he was smiling. 'The woods have named you. Now you are truly one of us.'

Chapter Thirty-Four
TRIBUS

Juba and Castor were leading their ponies through dense woods, going towards the campfire smoke in the next valley.

'The woods end up ahead,' said Castor over his shoulder. 'Let's leave the ponies here, out of sight.'

Juba nodded and draped his pony's reins over a low branch of hazel.

He came up behind Castor, who had found a good view of the source of the smoke: a camp on the grassy slope of a hill across a small valley. The sun was sinking towards the tops of the trees on the far ridge. It was only two weeks after the spring equinox. Juba knew that meant they were looking almost due west.

He counted perhaps thirty-six tents on the grassy hill, arranged not in rows, as a Roman camp would be, but in circles of five or six around fires. Long-haired Britons were coming in and out of the tents, some sat near the fires preparing food. A tent of blue canvas, bigger than the others, sat on a higher part of ground near the edge of some woods. It was flanked by two smaller goatskin tents.

'That looks more like our uprising,' murmured Castor. 'Nearly forty tents.'

'Tribal groups?' whispered Juba.

'Looks like it,' said Castor. 'Those men on the left are wearing the same blue, yellow and green as people in your Belgae village.'

'But I don't recognise any of them,' said Juba. 'They must be from one of the other Belgae villages. Look!' He pointed. 'I'm sure that's the colour of the Trinovantes. And those other men with the long faces and dark hair look like a Durotrigan woman we saw at Aquae Sulis.'

'And those ones have reddish hair like Bouda,' added Castor. He looked at Juba. 'My cousin Flavia was right. The Tribes of the Beaver are uniting!'

'Tribes of the Beaver?' Juba frowned. 'What are you talking about?'

'It's something Flavia Gemina invented to help her remember which tribes are which here in southern Britannia. I'll show you.'

Castor took a twig and drew an outline in the earth at the foot of their bush. 'Wait,' he said, scrubbing out part of it. 'They have quite big heads. There. That's better. Can you see what I've drawn?'

'Is it a beaver facing right?'

'Yes. It's roughly the shape of the southern part of Britannia. Now, the top of his head is the Iceni tribe.'

'Bouda's tribe,' murmured Juba.

Castor nodded. 'And the bottom of his head, his lower jaw, is the Trinovantes. Of course it's a huge simplification,' he said. 'As you know, you can get a Belgae village just three miles away from a Dobunni one.'

Juba nodded. 'Where's Londinium?'

'Here, where the beaver's front paw meets his chin,' said Castor, and made more marks dividing the beaver. 'His front paw is the area of the Cantici and his following paw is the Regni.'

He scratched a letter C in one paw and R in the other. 'The heart of the beaver is the Catuvellauni tribe.'

Juba nodded. 'Those three tribes have been friendly to Rome the longest.' He parted branches to look back at the camp. 'And I don't see any of them there.'

Castor continued making marks in the dust and putting a letter in each portion. 'The beaver's back is the Dobunni, his stomach is the Atrebates, his bowels the Belgae, and his rump the Durotriges. Finally, his big fat tail is the Dumnonii.'

'I'm not sure what the Dumnonii look like,' said Juba, taking another look at the camp, 'but we've got those other four tribes.'

'Which makes sense,' said Castor. 'I think we're right about here, where the territory of the Dubonni meet the Atrebates, Catuvellauni and Belgae.' He used the twig to point to the centre of the beaver's body, nearer the top than the bottom.

Juba looked out at the slope. 'So we have warriors from six or seven different tribes gathered together. Just as Flavia Gemina said: a Druid-led uprising.' In the stillness he heard a blackbird give its warning cry somewhere in the woods behind them. 'But where,' he murmured, 'is the Druid who's supposed to be leading them?'

Even as he spoke, he saw someone emerge from the largest tent: the blue one by the woods. The man had flowing white robes, long white hair and three blue snakes for a beard.

Juba swallowed hard.

Even from this distance, he could see the man's penetrating black gaze, and he shrank back as the eyes looked in his direction.

'There's our enemy!' Juba whispered in a choked voice. 'Right in front of us!'

'And also,' said a voice in Brittonic, 'right behind you.'

Juba whirled to see two dark-haired Britons aiming light javelins at his chest.

He managed to choke out the word 'Pax!' and put up his palms to show he held no weapons. Then he looked around for his companion.

But Castor was nowhere to be seen.

Chapter Thirty-Five
FASCINATIO

Fronto, Vindex and Cicatrix found the strange village in the clearing thanks to the cheerful sound of flute and drums.

'Doesn't sound like bloodthirsty Druids,' growled Cicatrix, 'and we're still disguised as Batavian sausage-sellers, but let's be wary all the same.' He used his heels to nudge his horse into motion and led the way down a gentle slope through a leafy green tunnel with colours glowing like gemstones at the far end. The colours turned out to be tents.

As they rode into the clearing, Fronto saw an oak tree fluttering with bits of yarn and scraps of brass. At its base were four boys and two girls of about his age. They were dancing around someone wearing a bird-feather cloak. One of the boys was patting a drum slung across his body and the most beautiful girl Fronto had ever seen was playing a flute. She had long silver-blonde hair and a headband made of a plaited blue ribbon.

Then the figure in the bird-feather cloak turned and he saw her face.

'Ursula!' he cried.

The music stopped abruptly.

'Fronto!' His sister squealed with delight, broke out of the circle and ran to him. Her arms were tight around him the moment he dismounted. It was wonderful to feel her safe and solid. But strange to feel the silky feathers of her cloak.

'Are you all right?' he cried. 'They said you were abducted.'

'I was recruited!' she cried. 'Look! They let me wear the cloak of honour!' She spread out her arms and twirled. On her shoulder Meer meowed as she attempted to cling to the slippery feathers. 'I've never felt so alive!' cried Ursula.

'*Carpe diem!*' agreed Loquax, flying down to her other shoulder from the colourful oak tree.

'You won't believe it, Fronto,' Ursula cried, 'but the trees and the bushes are alive, too!'

'The trees are alive?' Fronto looked closer. Something about her was wrong; her eyes were too bright.

He lowered his voice. 'Ursula, what have you been doing for three days?' he said. 'Who are these people? Have they bewitched you?'

'They're studying to be Druids!' cried Ursula happily. 'Vindex!' She hugged him too, and then looked at Cicatrix.

'Ursula, this is Cicatrix, my commanding officer,' said Fronto. 'He came to help us rescue you.'

Ursula threw her arms around the startled centurion, whose scowl turned to a lopsided smile.

'Hello, Cicatrix!' Ursula laughed. 'Thank you for coming but I don't want to be rescued! I love it here! The goddess sent me here. Look who I found!'

With a dramatic flourish she swung both arms out towards the young dancers, breathing hard.

'This is Sneezing Vole and One Ember and Standing Hawk. Those beautiful girls are Nimble Tree and Dancing Wren and best of all, this is Raven!' She ran to a dark-haired youth and grabbed his arm. 'Look!' she squealed, pulling him forward. 'Look who kidnapped me!'

'Castor?' said Fronto in disbelief.

'No!' Ursula laughed. 'Look again! His name is Raven's Wing but we call him Raven for short. His hair is longer than Castor's and he has a little tiny scar on his left eyebrow. But apart from that . . . Isn't it amazing? That's why I wasn't afraid when he pulled me into the chariot,' she added. 'I thought it was Castor! But it was his *identical twin*!'

Fronto stepped closer to peer at Castor's uncanny lookalike.

The dark-haired boy gave a rueful smile. 'I think your sister drank too much potion.' He spoke Latin with an accent.

Fronto glanced at Ursula. 'I'm *sure* she drank too much potion. But you do look exactly like our friend Castor.'

Vindex had also come closer to peer at him. 'Where are you from?' he asked in Brittonic.

'I'm from the north,' replied Raven in the same language. 'From the tribe of Corieltauvi.'

Fronto looked at Vindex. 'I've never even heard of that tribe.'

'I have,' said Vindex. 'And it makes sense: he speaks Brittonic perfectly but with a northern accent.'

'You're right, Ursula.' Fronto shook his head. 'It must be Castor's long-lost brother! But he never said it was his twin.'

'But it had to be!' cried Ursula. 'Think about it! How else would he know his brother had been spotted? People must have told Castor they'd seen him at places he'd never been. That's how he knew his brother was his identical twin. That must be how he knew his brother was here in Britannia.'

'I don't believe you,' said Raven in Brittonic. 'There were twin priests at Aquae Sulis. They didn't look exactly alike.'

164

'You were at Aquae Sulis?' cried Ursula. 'Were you there six months ago? On the last day of October?'

'Of course,' said Raven. 'I was an apprentice priest there, helping my father, who is a haruspex.'

'Your father?' Ursula and Vindex spoke at the same time. It took Fronto another few moments to realise the significance of this.

When understanding finally dawned, he frowned at Castor's twin. 'But your father was a Roman,' he said. 'From Ostia.'

'Roman?' Raven tossed his hair away from his face. 'There is no way my father could be Roman. My father was born Iceni, but grew up among the Corieltauvi. His name is Volisius, but he calls himself Snakebeard.'

Chapter Thirty-Six
BELLATORES

The two dark-haired warriors bringing Juba into the camp were Durotriges. He could tell by their woollen trousers with the orange and brown stripes.

As they moved up the grassy slope, some Belgae men sitting around a fire jumped up. Some started to go for their swords or spears, then sat back on the grass, watching with wary eyes. Juba noticed they weren't only staring at him, but also at his captors. He remembered that the fair-haired Belgae and dark-haired Durotriges were enemies.

The two Durotrigan warriors glared back and prodded Juba roughly towards the biggest tent, which was guarded by a bare-chested Briton with bushy red hair.

'Found a spy,' said one of the warriors. 'Tell the Archdruid.' The guard grunted, stuck his head through the flap and said something.

Hearing a man's reply, the guard held the flap open.

Juba went in.

The man seated cross-legged before a game board had white hair, skin and robes but strong sunlight shining through the coloured tent washed him in blue. Juba knew that only the three plaits of his beard were really blue.

The blue-tinted man looked up and smiled. 'Salve, Lucius Domitius Juba,' he said in lightly accented Latin. 'It is an honour to meet you.' He had capped the end of each beard plait with a golden snakehead and these clicked softly as he rose to his feet. Juba guessed he was between fifty and sixty, but his dark eyes were as keen and intelligent as a man half his age.

Juba's mouth was dry but he managed to ask, 'Who are you? And how do you know my name?'

'I am Snakebeard, the Archdruid. And how could I not know your name? My gods sent you to help me. You and your sister and the girl named Bouda.'

'Are they here?' Juba looked around the blue-tinted space. He could see a wooden chest, a long bronze war horn and a bed of furs, but no girls. 'If you've hurt them . . .' He clenched his fists and took a step forward but strong arms pushed him roughly down.

'Show respect, Roman dog!' growled the red-haired guard in Brittonic.

Juba found himself on his knees, one arm wrenched painfully behind his back.

'Let him up,' said Snakebeard with a faint smile. And to Juba, 'Your sister Ursula and friend Bouda are both well and unharmed,' he said. 'You'll see them soon. First, I would like to know how you made an enemy of Rome's Emperor.'

'Why should I tell you anything?' snarled Juba as he struggled to his feet. He was stiff, frightened and alone. Castor had fled like a coward and abandoned him. Now he was unarmed and helpless, surrounded by two hundred hostile warriors.

Snakebeard went to a leather satchel hanging from one of the tent frames. He fished in it and brought out a familiar-looking leather belt with a coin pouch on the left and the sheath for a dagger on the right.

'My belt and dagger!' Juba stared in disbelief. 'They were stolen from me half a year ago at the baths of Aquae Sulis.'

'Yes,' said Snakebeard, his dark eyes glinting. 'My agent was over-enthusiastic. It was cruel to take your clothes and belt, as well as your cloak.'

'It was you?' Juba gasped. 'You're the one who stole my clothes? Then you know about—' He stopped himself just in time.

'The hidden treasure?' Snakebeard laughed. 'Of course we do. It's an old trick to sew coins and gems into the seam of a cloak. How do you think I paid for this gathering?'

Juba stared stupidly. 'What?'

Snakebeard went to the tent flap and pulled it back. The door framed a view of the tents, fires and warriors. 'You can't start a rebellion without money,' he said. 'Messengers had to be sent out. Grain bought. Animals slaughtered. Cloth woven. White cloaks are almost as costly as purple, you know.'

'What?' said Juba again. He still did not understand.

Snakebeard smiled patiently. 'In the past,' he said, 'all the tribes joined together to support the Druidic priesthood. Now that we no longer exist, there was no way to pay for the resources needed to train the next generation. I had enough to start a school, but your gems funded an uprising.'

Juba stared out at the warriors around their tents. He felt numb. 'The gems in my cloak paid for this uprising?'

Snakebeard held up three fingers. 'Three gems, to be specific. I have many left.'

'Those gems belonged to my father!' Juba blinked back angry tears. 'He and my mother gave their lives to protect us and provide for us.'

'And you will be provided for,' said Snakebeard, 'as long as you don't resist me.' He handed Juba his belt with the ivory handled dagger still in its sheath. 'Here. Take this as a gesture of my goodwill. Come and eat. I can smell our food.'

He led the way out into the slanting sunlight of late afternoon.

For a moment Juba considered plunging his dagger into the old man's back, but he was surrounded by two hundred warriors, all eager for blood. So he left the dagger in its scabbard and strapped on his familiar belt.

Outside, Juba glanced up at the ridge where he and Castor had hidden a half hour earlier. Was he there? Watching perhaps?

'Hear that?' said Snakebeard, cocking his head.

Juba could hear nothing but the crackle of fires and low conversation. Even this died away as the warriors looked at Snakebeard.

'I don't hear anything,' Juba replied.

'Exactly,' said Snakebeard. 'No birds, no animals, not even any wind. They say this place is haunted by the ghosts of eighty thousand Britons.' Snakebeard gazed down the slope towards a broad Roman road, just visible behind shrubs and trees. 'This was where Queen Boudica suffered her first and final defeat.'

'But nobody knows exactly where that was,' said Juba. 'Suetonius Paulinus covered over the battlefield and all traces of it.'

'It is true that Paulinus took away most of the bodies and buried them in a pit,' said Snakebeard. 'And it is true that they say the site is unknown. That is because they do not want us Britons to gain courage from this site. But I know that this is the place.'

'How can you know?'

'Because I was there.'

'You were there?' Juba looked at the Druid. 'At the massacre of Boudica's army?'

'Yes. When I was your sister's age. Perhaps a little older. Perhaps Bouda's age: twelve. She is twelve, is she not?'

'I'm not sure.'

'Then let's ask her,' said Snakebeard in a different tone of voice. 'Bouda!' he called. 'Bouda, come out and see who has come to visit.' He turned to the small tent flanking his.

A moment later the flap of the tent was pulled back and Bouda stepped out into the fading light of late afternoon. She wore a nettle-cloth cloak of pure white and her copper hair had feathers and acorns woven into it.

Juba's spirits soared when he saw that she was unharmed and well. He took a smiling step forward, but his smile faltered when he saw a familiar jewel in the fibula that fastened the neck of her long white cloak. He recognised it as one of the gems from his father's birrus Britannicus.

'Traitor!' he spat. 'I might have guessed. You're the one who stole my cloak at Aquae Sulis! How long have you been spying for Snakebeard?'

Chapter Thirty-Seven
APOLOGIA

Bouda glared at Juba. 'How could I steal your cloak at Aquae Sulis? You left it in the men's changing room.'

Snakebeard raised an eyebrow. 'I see there is little trust between you. It wasn't Bouda who took your cloak,' he added, 'but my son, Raven.'

Juba glanced at Snakebeard and then said to Bouda, 'So you're not working for him?'

Bouda lifted her chin. 'I wasn't before,' she said, 'but the past few days have convinced me.'

Juba felt sick. 'Convinced you of what?'

'That the Roman oppressor must be crushed if we Britons are to regain our freedom!'

Juba stared at the grass so that Snakebeard could not read his expression. Ever since he had first met Bouda she had loved the Roman way of life. Had Snakebeard really convinced her to hate Rome? Or was she pretending? He knew she would do anything to survive.

'Have you seen Ursula?' he asked.

'I told you,' said Snakebeard. 'You will see her tomorrow.' To Bouda he said, 'Time for us to eat.' He raised his voice and directed it towards Bouda's tent. 'Girls!'

Two muscular girls came out of the tent. They wore leather breast-bands, short woollen kilts and grim expressions. Juba tried not to stare at the tattoos on their arms and the knives in their belts. If Bouda had truly gone over to Snakebeard then why did she need guards? A flicker of hope kindled in his heart. Maybe she was just pretending.

'Come, sit!' Snakebeard said to Juba. 'I want to tell you more about our plans. Perhaps I can convince you to join our fight to expel the Roman from this island.'

'Why should I want to help you do that?' asked Juba.

Snakebeard tipped his head back. 'Are you telling me you are still loyal to the man who killed your parents and confiscated your property?'

'You're the one who confiscated my property,' snapped Juba. 'When you had my cloak stolen.'

Snakebeard was about to reply when a warrior with tattoos and a torc hurried up. 'Sir,' he cried. 'My scouts have confirmed that a vexillation bearing the standard of the governor is on the road towards Londinium. They're spending the night in Lactodurum and should pass by here sometime tomorrow morning.'

'Perfect!' cried Snakebeard. 'The gods are with us!'

He turned to Juba. 'You're lucky. You're about to hear the speech I've been working on for the past few days.' He threw out his arms so that his white-cloaked body formed a fluttering square. Gather round, warriors!' he shouted.

Warriors got up from their fires and came to stand on the grassy slope below him.

'Welcome to all you representatives of the southern tribes of this island,' cried Snakebeard in clear Brittonic. 'You Iceni and you Dumnonii have come the furthest: Welcome. To you

Dobunni, Silures and Durotriges: Welcome. I welcome also warriors of the Atrebates and those from the Trinovantes. Not forgetting the Belgae. And I am happy to see some of you have brought female warriors with you. The Romans hate that!'

This raised a laugh among the warriors and Juba heard feminine war whoops.

Scanning the crowd, Juba was surprised to see an Atrebate woman with matted hair the colour of oakwood and a pretty Durotrigan girl with black hair pulled up in a topknot like Bouda's guards. They were cheering and banging their spears against their small round shields along with the men.

'Boudica—' began Snakebeard. And Juba was surprised to hear another deafening cheer.

Snakebeard raised his right hand in the classic gesture for silence. Instantly the warriors on the slope were quiet and he continued.

'Thirty-five years,' he said, 'when I was this girl's age, I saw Boudica rise up against the Romans.' Here he put his hand on Bouda's arm.

Juba wasn't certain, but he thought he saw her flinch.

Snakebeard continued in his raspy voice, 'I rode in one of the wagons of the supply train with my mother and little sister. Like many other families we followed our warriors, who had destroyed the Roman towns of Camulodunum, Londinium and Verulamium. Tens of thousands of them were on their way north to meet the governor and destroy him, too! We wanted to watch Queen Boudica and her brave warriors deal the final death blow.'

Snakebeard swept his left arm towards the woods.

'The Romans were drawn up here, in the very place where I am standing now. My family and I were down there on the road. We thought we had the Romans trapped! See? Thick woods behind me, and on both sides, widening towards the road. And we were at the bottom. We had them, like a badger in a basket.'

He looked around slowly, his eyes as black as night.

'But we were mistaken,' he said. 'It was not the Romans who were trapped. It was us. Our first line of warriors were cut down by their slings and arrows, and our second line, too. The Romans stood in silence, a wall of shields. Although there were tens of thousands of us, we could not outflank them because of the woods. And because they stood strong on the narrowest part, we could only throw so many men at them at a time.'

His voice cracked but he took a breath and went on. 'Then at last they attacked. They advanced downhill in ordered ranks, like a slow but steady landslide crushing the bodies of our dead and wounded. Our warriors tried to retreat, so that they could regroup, but our supply wagons formed a barrier far more solid than the woods. The Romans cut them down and then they started on us.'

As Snakebeard told how the Romans began to kill women and children, Juba saw that Bouda's chin was trembling and her eyes were full of tears.

The warriors on the slope were utterly silent as Snakebeard told them how he had become the only British survivor.

He told how he had squirmed out from under a blood-soaked pile of bodies as the Romans ruthlessly cut the throats of those still living.

'I ran into the woods,' he said and his strong voice was now husky with pain. 'I was like a half-wild creature with no thoughts but to escape. For a year, maybe two, I had no words. I lived on bugs and worms. On mushrooms and berries. On leaves and bark. Every day I swam to wash the blood away but I never felt clean.'

Snakebeard lowered his head and when he raised it again Juba saw the pain replaced by triumph.

'An old Druid found me and taught me to hear the gods. And one day the great thunder god Taranis came to me in a dream. "You will only be free," he said, "when you have killed every Roman in the land. When you have spilled as much blood of theirs as they spilled of ours. I will send messengers," said Taranis. "When the Three Hooded Ones come to bring gifts to the Great Goddess then you will know your time is near."'

A prickle of awe made Juba shiver. Were he and his siblings under the control of some barbarian god or goddess?

Snakebeard lowered his voice but in the absolute silence they could all hear him. 'Sometime tomorrow morning,' he said, 'the governor of Britannia will pass along the road you can see. The very road upon which so much British blood was spilled. My scouts have told me that he is travelling with just a few members of his entourage and a mere half century of soldiers. There are not many of them and there are not many of us. But if we can kill the governor's bodyguard and sacrifice him to Taranis,' he said, 'it will strike terror into the hearts of the Romans and encourage the tribes of Britannia everywhere. It will be the first step in a new uprising where all the tribes will unite.'

Snakebeard turned towards Bouda. Juba saw her eyes widen but she barely flinched when he grasped her shoulders from behind. With his blue-bearded, black-eyed gorgon-face, he looked like a proud but terrifying father standing behind her.

'This girl,' said Snakebeard, his voice strong again, 'claims that she is the great-granddaughter of Boudica.' He lifted a plait of her hair. 'See how red her hair is? How fierce her eyes?'

There was an excited murmur among the warriors on the green slope.

Snakebeard took a breath. 'Even if she had not told me herself, I would have recognised her. For she looks exactly like her famous ancestor, Queen Boudica, whom I myself beheld with these eyes. But where Boudica failed,' he continued at the top of his voice, 'her descendant will not. This girl named Bouda will speak to you tomorrow and inspire you to victory.'

Juba looked at Bouda in astonishment. The warriors were buzzing with excitement, until the Archdruid's next statement silenced them once more.

'Boudica's name will be forgotten!' cried Snakebeard. 'And why?'

He paused dramatically. 'Because another name will supersede hers. History will remember the girl who vanquished the Romans and united the tribes of this island to become Queen Bouda!'

Here he lifted up her right arm. 'Say it with me!' he cried. 'Bouda! *Bouda! BOUDA!*'

Bouda's pale cheeks flushed pink and her green eyes flashed. The former beggar girl and cutpurse was being cheered as a Queen of Britannia.

Juba felt sick. His own gems were funding the uprising against Rome, and the girl he had taken under his wing was to be its figurehead.

Chapter Thirty-Eight
GEMINI

It was evening in Mistletoe Oak and Fronto was just helping himself to another bowlful of stew from a bronze cauldron beneath the oak when he heard his name being shouted. Fronto and the others turned to see a figure in a dark grey hooded cloak crashing down through shrubs into the clearing.

They all rose to their feet and Cicatrix drew his dagger. But Fronto put his hand on the centurion's arm. He had recognised Castor, the young ship owner who had brought them to Britannia.

'Fronto!' cried Castor. 'Thank the gods you're here! Hostile warriors have captured Juba, and Bouda's with them, too! They're going to attack the governor tomorrow and do something terrible to him. A terrifying Druid with snakes for a beard is leading them—' He came skidding to a stop about twenty paces from Raven. He stood staring, open-mouthed. His hood was back and there was a twig in his dark hair.

'Castor!' cried Ursula. 'Look! We found your long-lost brother!'

Fronto squinted in disbelief. Raven's hooded cloak was bone white and Castor's was charcoal grey, almost black, but apart from that, they were identical. Both had dark hair, pale skin and the same perfect profile. They were even the same height.

Ursula was clapping her hands, but the others were staring open-mouthed. Suddenly the girl with the curly brown hair fainted and would have knocked the stewpot off the coals if the red-headed youth had not caught her.

'Philadelphus?' Castor's voice was husky. 'Can it really be you?' He took a step forward, his arms outstretched.

White-cloaked Raven took a step back. 'Who's Philadelphus?' He frowned at Castor. 'And who are you?'

Fronto looked at Raven. How could he not recognise his own brother?

'Can't you see?' said the blonde girl. 'Can't you see who it is?'

Raven frowned and shook his head, his anger mixed with puzzlement.

Then Ursula clapped her hands. 'Raven!' she cried. 'When was the last time you looked in a mirror? Or your reflection in a water bucket? When was the last time you saw yourself?'

Raven scowled. 'Maybe when I was nine or ten,' he said.

The red-headed youth pointed at Castor. 'You look like him,' he said.

'I look like him?' Raven's lip curled in disbelief. 'I look like that pretty-boy Roman?'

Cicatrix gave a snort of laughter and put his dagger back in its sheath.

'Yes!' cried the curly-haired girl. 'You look exactly like him!'

They all nodded, and Fronto said, 'You're like the mythical twins, Castor and Pollux.' And for the first time it occurred to him that Castor might not be Castor's real name.

Castor lowered his arms but took another hesitant step forward. 'I have been seeking you for over a year,' he said. 'Since I first learned of your existence.'

'No,' said Raven, taking a step back. 'No, I don't believe it.'

'Your real name is Philadelphus and my real name is Soter, which means saviour in Greek. You speak Greek, don't you?'

Raven scowled and gave a curt nod. 'My mother is Greek.'

Castor's eyes grew wide. 'Is her name Lydia?'

It was Raven's turn to stare. 'How do you know that?'

'Jonathan's theory was right,' muttered Castor. To Raven he said, 'The woman called Lydia was your wet-nurse, hired to suckle you after her own baby died. Your real mother wasn't Greek. She was a Jewess from Judea. Her name was Miriam. And your father was a Roman named Gaius Flavius Geminus.'

'I've never heard of such a thing as a Jewess!' cried Raven. 'My mother was a Greek slave who hated the Romans as much as my father does.'

'Castor!' Ursula cried. 'He thinks his father is Snakebeard!'

Castor stared. 'The Druid I just saw with snakes for a beard? You call him father?'

Raven nodded.

Castor took a deep breath. 'Phil—, I mean Raven,' he said. 'The governor and his entourage will be passing this way tomorrow. There may be a woman called Flavia Gemina travelling with them. She is our cousin. Her father was the twin brother of our father. Just as you and I are twins. If you help this so-called Snakebeard with his plan, you will be responsible for killing your own flesh and blood.'

'No.' Raven turned away. 'You're trying to trick me. I'm not Roman and I don't look like you.'

Cicatrix stepped forward and addressed Castor. 'Where are the warriors now, and how many are there?' he asked in a low growl.

'They have a camp a mile and a half that way,' said Castor.

'There are about two hundred warriors from eight different tribes, armed with javelins and arrows.' He was looking at Raven, whose back was still turned.

Cicatrix nodded. 'They probably mean to attack from the cover of bushes and trees,' he said. 'Almost impossible to defend yourself against such an ambush. By the time the troops are drawn up, the enemy has melted away. And for a small vexillation it means death.'

Fronto looked at Castor. 'Did you say Juba is in the warrior camp with Snakebeard?'

Castor nodded. 'Bouda, too. She's going to give a speech to the warriors tomorrow.'

'One of us has to warn the governor!' said Fronto.

'Wait!' Cicatrix rubbed his big chin. 'If you tell the governor that a gathering of Britons are waiting to ambush him he might order the massacre of everyone in every village within a five mile radius.' He glanced at Vindex. 'Maybe more.'

'Why would he do that?' gasped Ursula.

'To keep the Pax Romana,' said Vindex and Fronto together.

Cicatrix nodded. 'The thing every governor fears most is another uprising like the one in the time of Boudica,' he said. 'Apart from causing thousands of deaths, Domitian would have his head.'

'Why can't Britons and Romans be friends?' asked Ursula. 'Like the trees and the bushes tell us?'

'Yes!' said the blonde girl. The red-headed boy turned to Castor's twin brother. 'Raven,' he said. 'You are the one who's always telling us there must be a better way than violence. You heard the song of the trees and the bushes. They sing of life, not death.'

'And look!' The hawk-nosed boy gestured at Castor. 'A

Roman and a Briton who look exactly alike. Is there any clearer sign that we are all brothers at heart, and that we should seek peace not war?'

'Wise words,' said Castor with a gentle smile. Then he opened his arms to Raven. 'Come,' he said. 'Embrace me, and call me brother.'

With both arms held stiffly at his side and his fists clenched, Raven stared at the ground. 'You've just told me that my whole life is a lie . . . That my father is not my father and my mother is not my mother. You tell me I am a member of a race of men I have been taught to hate. And you expect me to embrace you and call you brother, but . . .'

He slowly raised his head and Fronto saw his handsome face contorted by anguish. 'I don't want to embrace you. I want to *kill* you!'

And with that, he threw himself at Castor.

Chapter Thirty-Nine
CONSILIUM

Ursula screamed as the twins rolled on the ground. Raven was trying to punch Castor, who refused to fight back, but used his cloaked arms to cover his head. Their black and white cloaks became tangled and made it hard for Raven to land a blow.

Suddenly all the fight went out of Raven. He slumped with his forehead to the ground, weeping.

Breathing hard, Castor leaned forward to embrace his brother.

'Don't touch me!' Raven used the flat of his hand to shove Castor away and rose unsteadily to his feet. 'I have to talk to her! I have to get her to tell me the truth.'

Cicatrix shook his big head.

'Sorry, son,' he said, 'but we can't let you go. You might warn Snakebeard.'

Raven gave the centurion a bitter smile. 'I won't warn him. I've been plotting against him for the last month, since he came up with the idea of starting a new rebellion.' He looked at the others. 'They'll tell you.'

Nimble Tree nodded. 'It's true. Snakebeard taught us how to make the potion and go into the woods,' she said. 'But the trees taught us that violence is not the way. Raven convinced us to pray for peace tomorrow, rather than victory.'

'Then stay with us and help us stop him!' cried Ursula, taking a step forward.

'No!' Raven shook his head and stared at the ground. 'I have to see my mother. To find out the truth.'

'You only have to look at your reflection to know it's true!' cried Ursula. She looked around. 'Doesn't anyone have a mirror? Or a piece of polished tin?'

Cicatrix pulled out a dagger, polished to mirror brightness and held it up.

But Raven refused to look.

'I need to hear the truth from her,' he repeated. He took off his white cloak and held it out. 'Who will trade cloaks with me? I don't want to wear this any more.'

Castor immediately stepped forward. 'I will trade.'

'No.' Raven averted his head. 'I don't want anything of yours.'

Ursula was surprised to see Fronto step forward. 'Have my cloak,' he said. 'It is beaver skin and very warm.'

Raven hesitated a moment, then gave a curt nod and took it, handing over his white cloak in exchange.

This time Cicatrix did not protest when Castor's twin went to the stable tent and led out the biggest pony, a shaggy chestnut mare.

'Raven, don't leave. Please.' Castor took a step towards his brother, but Nimble Tree put her hand on his arm. 'Let him go,' she whispered, as Raven kicked his mount into a gallop. 'His world has been turned upside down.'

When the hoofbeats of Raven's horse had faded into the distance, Cicatrix turned to Castor. 'Tell us about this gathering of warriors.'

Castor was still looking at the path Raven had taken.

'Tell us!' roared Cicatrix.

Castor gave his head a small shake as if to clear it. 'Snakebeard has Juba and Bouda,' he said. 'I'm not sure if she's working for him or just pretending. He's promised to make her a queen, like that famous warrioress: Boudica.'

'The traitor!' hissed Ursula. 'She'll do anything for money.'

'No!' said Fronto fiercely. 'I don't believe it. If it seems she's gone over to Snakebeard then it's him she's betraying, not us.'

'You really like her, don't you?' Ursula whispered.

Fronto nodded. 'She's the reason I joined the army,' he admitted. 'She's the reason I was trying to learn how to be brave.'

'We need to stop the governor's vexillation from coming this way,' said Cicatrix. 'And I am the only one they will trust. It's too dark now, but tomorrow I will ride out at dawn. I can tell the governor a bridge is out and advise him to take an alternate route. Then I'll ride back to help you take down Snakebeard. Without a spokesman the tribes might drift apart.'

Castor nodded. 'I heard Snakebeard speak tonight. The warriors don't know him well; some of them heard him for the first time this evening. There's no great loyalty yet and no sense of unity. Some of the tribes would fight each other if provoked. If we can silence Snakebeard, the warriors might disperse and go back to their tribes.'

Vindex had been silent but now he spoke up. 'Do you have to go, sir? We need you here to command us. You know strategy.'

Fronto nodded his agreement.

Cicatrix's ugly face creased into a frown. 'Then how will we warn the governor?'

'An arrow!' cried Fronto suddenly. 'One of us can stand

somewhere with a view of the road. If they come before we've stopped Snakebeard then we'll fire a warning arrow.'

'I have some fire arrows in my quiver,' said Vindex.

Cicatrix gave him an approving nod. 'Good idea. The warning will be enough to stop them but they won't know why. No retaliation.' He looked at the five young Druids. 'You say you want peace?'

They all nodded.

'If I promise to take Snakebeard alive, and that nobody else will be harmed, will you help me? The alternative is war with Rome and you know that will mean terrible bloodshed.'

One Ember and Standing Hawk looked at each other and nodded. 'Snakebeard wants us to stand and call down curses on the Romans,' said One Ember. 'Raven convinced us to pray for peace not war. We can still do that. We can use the green power of the trees to calm the red particles of their anger.' He gestured at Nimble Tree and Dancing Wren. 'These two are like water on coals.'

'I don't have a clue what you're talking about,' said Cicatrix 'But I trust you.'

'So we need to silence Snakebeard,' said Ursula, 'but also to rescue Juba!'

'And Bouda,' said Fronto. 'And the sooner the better.'

'Bouda's going to speak to the warriors tomorrow,' Castor reminded them.

Ursula's heart was suddenly pounding. 'I have a plan,' she said. 'I think I know how to silence Snakebeard. And if Bouda's on our side, I know how to convince the warriors not to fight tomorrow. And I also know how to get into the camp tonight to rescue Juba—'

They were all staring at her, wide-eyed.

She looked at Castor. 'But you have to help us. Without you we can't do anything.'

'Of course,' said Castor. 'I'll help if I can.'

'Not so fast, lad,' said Cicatrix. 'She's just a little girl and she might be drunk or bewitched or something.' He folded his arms and looked at Ursula. 'What is your plan?'

Ursula told them.

When she had finished, everyone was looking at her in awe.

'It is a mad plan,' said the ugly centurion. He looked at Castor. 'But if your twin doesn't show up to ruin things it might just work.' Then he looked at Ursula. 'Are you really brave enough to go through with it?'

'I am,' said Ursula, lifting her chin.

Cicatrix nodded. 'Let's go through it one more time, so everybody knows what they're doing. Then let's go; there is not a moment to be lost.'

Chapter Forty
LUNA

An almost half moon was rising when Ursula led Castor into the Druid war camp. They came forward openly: Ursula with her hands bound, and Castor behind her in the white hooded cloak that had belonged to his twin.

'I hope this works,' muttered Castor. 'There are so many things that could go wrong.'

'You look exactly like him,' she said. 'The guards have to let Snakebeard's own son into the camp.'

'But my Brittonic is not as good as his.'

'Just whisper!' said Ursula. 'It's hard to tell someone's accent when they whisper.'

'I always knew you were brave.' Castor kept his voice low. 'But I never thought you could be this bold.'

Ursula's heart soared at his words.

'Don't smile,' he whispered. 'You're supposed to be my prisoner.'

A moment later a dark shape moved forward: a bare-chested warrior with long hair and a javelin.

'Oh, it's you,' he said, before Castor could identify himself. 'I thought you lot were coming tomorrow. Your father is in the woods, praying to the god of war. Shall I take you to him?'

'No need,' said Castor. 'I need to talk to the prisoner: the dark-skinned boy?'

'He's in the tent to the right of Snakebeard's.' The warrior jerked his head towards the higher part of the slope.

Castor prodded Ursula forwards.

As they moved up the grassy slope Ursula could make out the embers of campfires and a few dark forms of men wrapped in animal skins or cloaks outside some tents.

At the highest point of the hill, nearly at the treeline, was a large tent flanked by two smaller ones. A female warrior stood outside the smaller tent on the right. Ursula stared. The girl wore a leather breast strap and a short woollen skirt. Her bare arms and legs were covered with tattooed spirals.

'Hello, Raven,' said the tattooed girl warrior when she saw Castor in his white cloak.

He nodded. 'I have another prisoner,' he said in a low voice.

The girl pulled back the flap. 'Do you want me to get your father?'

Castor shook his head.

She smiled at him and then glared at Ursula, who found it easy to look scared.

Inside the tent, a lamphorn gave off an orange light so dim that it took Ursula a few moments to make out two sleeping figures wrapped in sheepskins either side of a wooden chest. The further shape had to be Bouda, because the nearer one was her brother.

'Juba!' she whispered in Latin. 'Are you all right?'

He rubbed his eyes and sat up. 'Ursula! Castor!'

'Shhh!'

'How did you get in?'

Castor gave a sad smile. 'You won't believe it, but the twin

188

brother I've been seeking for the past year turns out to be Snakebeard's son.'

'What? Snakebeard is your father?'

'No, but Raven thinks he is.' Castor glanced back at the tent flap and lowered his voice. 'All I had to do was put on a white cloak and they think I'm him. It was Ursula's idea.'

'Are you here to get me out?'

'Not exactly,' said Castor. 'Your sister has a plan to stop Snakebeard. But for it to work we need Bouda. Is she with us?'

'Of course I am!' Bouda's tousled head rose up on the other side of the chest. In the dim orange light she seemed made of bronze. All except for those emerald-green eyes which she now narrowed at Ursula.

'I've been with you for half a year,' she hissed, 'and you *still* don't trust me?'

'Fronto trusts you,' said Ursula. 'And he convinced me to bring you in on our plan. If you betray us, all is lost. So you see, I do trust you.'

Chapter Forty-One
BOUDICA

At mid-morning of the next day, the sky was overcast and the mood tense. Nearly two hundred British warriors from eight different tribes had taken down their tents and hidden them in the woods. Now they were decorating each others' faces and torsos with black, red and blue warpaint.

Without the Archdruid's tents to draw the eye, the thick woods on the top of the ridge reminded Juba of the back wall of a Roman theatre. The shadowy gaps between the closely ranked beech and ash trees made a dozen places for the actors in this drama to enter or exit.

Juba stood beside his sister on the left of this outdoor stage with the two female warriors who guarded them.

To their right, at the centre of the stage, stood two light war chariots, painted and varnished. One was yoked to a team of white ponies and the other was pulled by blacks. The ponies stood patiently, dozing with their heads down.

On the slope below, some of the rival tribes had begun to taunt one another and a skirmish was brewing between the Durotriges and the Belgae when a war horn sounded. Its haunting boom called the warriors to attention on the damp green slope.

The horn sounded again, this time with a staccato finish, and a ragged cheer rose as Snakebeard emerged from between the trees. His hair was in spikes and he held a magnificent warhorn as tall as he was. Made of bronze and tin, the carnyx was shaped like a horse's head; it was designed to rise up above the heads of charging troops. The Druid's white robes fluttered in a chilly breeze that smelled of rain. Juba shivered and pulled his dark cloak tighter around his shoulders.

Snakebeard blew his horn for a third time and Juba heard a universal intake of breath as six young people in white cloaks emerged from gaps between the trees. Two were girls and four were boys about Fronto's age.

Their faces were painted with delicate blue spirals and on their heads they wore garlands of oak and ribbons. One of the girls was the willowy blonde Juba had seen in the strange village a mile and a half south. The other girl was also slender and beautiful but with a mass of curly brown hair. The hoods of their white cloaks were pulled back and Juba could see that the boys must be from different tribes. One had reddish-brown hair, one light brown hair and one curly dark brown hair. Juba stiffened when he realised that the fourth, with hair as straight and black as a raven's wing, was Castor.

'Don't worry,' murmured Ursula beside him. 'He looks exactly like the boy Snakebeard calls his son.'

As Snakebeard turned to look at them, Juba held his breath. If Snakebeard suspected something was amiss, then their whole plan would fall apart.

The six young Druids took up positions: three on the far side of the two chariots and three close to Juba and his sister. Then, facing the clusters of warriors on the slope below, they put up their hoods and bowed their heads.

Juba exhaled with relief as Snakebeard placed the horn on

the ground and stepped up onto the right hand chariot, the one with the white ponies. His white robes fluttered but the spikes of his hair were stiff.

'A few moments ago,' he began in a stern voice, 'a fight almost broke out between two tribes. This is what makes the Romans happy,' he said. 'They like it when you fight each other.'

The warriors looked up at him sullenly.

'When you fight each other,' continued Snakebeard, 'it leaves the Roman oppressor free to mine your metal, to shear your sheep, to collect your grain, to seize your hunting dogs. It leaves them free to get fat off the riches of this island.'

There was a low growl of angry agreement among the shivering warriors.

'What the Romans fear more than anything else,' continued Snakebeard in a carrying voice, 'is unity of the tribes. In the past, we Druids were the only ones who could bring the tribes together. That is why the Romans wiped them out. All but me. That is why I am here. To bring you all together!'

The warriors cheered.

Snakebeard spread out his arms to indicate the white-cloaked young Druids either side of him.

'These young Druids,' he said, 'are powerful magicians. As you attack, they will be praying for your protection and cursing the Romans.'

Another cheer, stronger this time.

'Last night in the forest,' continued Snakebeard, 'the god Taranis reminded me of the three signs he sent that our rebellion will be successful.'

All eyes were on the Archdruid.

'First came the Three Hooded Questers,' cried Snakebeard. 'Their appearance marks the beginning of a New Age. Second, was a cloak of jewels found in the sanctuary of the goddess that will fund our rebellion. Last but not least, the god sent us none other than the granddaughter of Boudica!' Snakebeard half turned on his chariot podium and gestured dramatically towards the woods.

Juba's jaw dropped as Bouda emerged from between two trees.

Her copper-coloured hair had been unplaited and fell in a cloud around her shoulders, almost to her waist. Fine blue spirals adorned each cheek. There was also a streak of blue paint beneath her black-outlined eyes.

She wore a checked garment of four colours: the orange of her hair, the green of her eyes, the blue of the woad and the white of her skin.

Juba swallowed hard. The Stoic philosophers taught that the eye sends out tiny particles. For the first time he knew what that meant. She was looking at him and he could feel the power of her green gaze.

From the grassy slope below, a huge cheer rose up from the warriors. Juba's heart was thudding as Bouda stepped up onto the chariot next to Snakebeard's.

The next part of the plan would be a diversion to lure Snakebeard into the forest, where Fronto would be waiting with soldiers. Juba still could not believe that his brother had been ready to desert and that his little sister had come up with this plan.

The warriors were still cheering Bouda when one of the white-robed youths bent as if suffering from cramps and then went into the forest. It was Castor, pretending to be Raven.

Snakebeard saw him go and frowned at the blonde girl and

the red-haired boy, as if to ask what was wrong. They shook their heads, as if to say they didn't know.

'Listen to what Boudica's granddaughter has to say!' announced Snakebeard. Then he stepped down off his chariot and followed Castor into the woods.

Only now did Bouda raise her right hand palm forward to ask for silence. She was in the chariot closest to where he was standing, the one hitched to a team of black ponies, and he could see her lifted hand tremble.

Juba held his breath. The first part of their plan had worked: Castor had lured Snakebeard into the woods, where he would be captured.

Everything now depended on Bouda. In the tent the night before, they had discussed what she would say, but part of him still wondered if he could trust her.

'My name is Bouda!' she cried, as the warriors grew quiet. 'I am the granddaughter of Queen Boudica, whose name you all know.'

There was another great cheer. Juba's heart was still thudding and he felt slightly queasy. All winter he had taught her the skills of oratory. Could she turn the mood of two hundred warriors, all hungry for blood?

'As you know,' Bouda continued in a carrying voice, 'the Roman governor and fifty soldiers will soon appear on the road behind you. The man who calls himself Snakebeard wants you to strike them down before they can respond.' She held up her hand to stop their cheers. 'When you have murdered the governor's friends and protectors, you will put their heads on spears. Later tonight we will take the governor to a sacred grove, put him in a wicker man and sacrifice him to Taranis, the god of sky and thunder!'

194

There was another great roar of approval.

'Tomorrow,' continued Bouda, 'after we have burned the governor, Snakebeard wants you to go into the surrounding villages and utterly destroy any British village with sympathy for the Romans.'

The cheer, when it came, was less enthusiastic.

Juba glanced towards the thick beech-woods, wondering if Snakebeard would come bursting out to stop her. But the tender leaves of spring cast a green veil over what might be happening in the woodland depths.

Everyone was focused on Bouda, so Juba turned back to her.

'If you go to a village and find wine instead of beer,' Bouda was saying, 'you are to kill all the inhabitants: men, women and children. If you find oil instead of butter, you will kill them all: men, women and children. If you find a single Roman god or goddess on their rings or on their brooches, you will kill them all: men, women and children.'

Juba nodded his approval at her use of the triplet. Her words were beginning to take effect. This time the warriors did not cheer. They were glancing at each other uneasily.

'Snakebeard told me what to say!' continued Bouda, 'But I am Boudica's granddaughter.' She raised her clenched fist. 'Nobody tells me what to say!'

There was an excited murmur, and a few warriors laughed.

'So what do you say, granddaughter of Boudica?' cried a blond moustached warrior near the front.

Bouda smiled and kept her voice strong: 'I say that most Britons want peace and most Romans want peace.' She paused for a moment to let this sink in. 'If you want to hunt, hunt bear! If you want to kill, kill boar or deer for food! Why must we kill one another?'

The murmuring grew louder. Some were nodding and others were shaking their heads.

The female guards were watching Ursula with open mouths and wide-eyes. When they moved closer to hear what she was saying, Juba grasped his sister's hand and pulled her into the woods behind them.

Once among the protective trees, he led the way to the right, weaving among the damp trunks on a silent carpet of bluebells.

'We have to find Fronto!' he whispered. 'We need him for our plan to work.'

'You don't have to tell me,' Ursula hissed. 'It's *my* plan!'

Chapter Forty-Two
GENII CUCULLATI

Fronto watched open-mouthed as Castor and Cicatrix tied Snakebeard to the ash tree. The Druid was struggling and although there was a gag in his mouth his blazing eyes spoke a thousand curses. Cicatrix saw Fronto standing frozen and gestured impatiently. 'Go!' he cried. 'Find your brother and sister as we planned. We've got this under control.'

Fronto nodded and glanced up at Vindex, perched near the top of the highest ash tree with a view of the road to the north. His friend had three fire-arrows and some burning embers and ash in a hollowed cow's horn. If the governor's party arrived before they had put their plan into effect he would fire red signal arrows, the colour of warning. Vindex also flapped his arm as if to say, Go!

As Fronto wove through trees towards the edge of the woods, he spotted two hooded forms coming towards him: his brother and sister. He ran to meet them.

'Don't hug me!' Ursula cried. 'Meer's down my front.'

Juba looked over Fronto's shoulder. 'Where's Snakebeard?'

'Back there at the foot of the lookout tree. Cicatrix and Castor have him bound and gagged.'

197

'Praise Jupiter!' breathed Juba. 'Come on! It's almost time for us to appear!'

As the three of them drew closer to the edge of the woods, they could hear Bouda clearly.

'I grew up a beggar in Londinium,' she was saying. 'I have seen that the Romans are human, like us. They have good qualities mixed with bad, just as we do. But I see a future where Romans live in roundhouses and British build country villas with corners and courtyards.'

The warriors on the slope shouted a mixture of insults and agreements.

'I see a future in which our gods mix with theirs, as they do at the great sanctuary of Sulis Minerva.'

This time there were more cheers than jeers.

'I see a future,' cried Bouda, 'where Britons drink Roman wine and Romans drink British beer!'

At this there was laughter and a roar of approval.

'Snakebeard speaks of how the gods sent him three signs,' continued Bouda in her clear voice. 'But the gods sent *me* three signs this morning.'

Instantly the Britons were silent; everyone was interested in signs from the gods.

'First!' cried Bouda, 'the Three Hooded Spirits. They have come with a message for us today.'

She turned and gestured.

Juba nodded. 'That's our cue! You lead, Fronto!'

Fronto led the way, shuffling dramatically with his hood pulled down low, praying that this time they *would* be recognised. He was wearing the charcoal grey cloak that Raven had refused to take, his brother wore the dark brown cloak that had once been his and Ursula was dressed as usual in her pine-green cloak.

A huge cheer showed that tales of the Three Hooded Questers were still being sung by bards in villages all over the province.

Then came something Fronto was not expecting: laughter.

Fronto knew that laughter dissolved anger, and this gave him courage.

'The Three Hooded Questers have been helping restore British children stolen by bickering tribes,' said Bouda, her voice still strong. 'And yet, they are ROMAN.'

She gestured dramatically. At her signal, Juba, Fronto and Ursula turned to face the troops and then pulled back their hoods to reveal faces which Fronto knew would look strange and exotic to the British.

Another universal gasp and then some ragged cheers.

'Next,' said Bouda, 'The Cloak of Jewels.' She held up a tawny birrus Britannicus.

'Praise the gods!' breathed Juba. 'She found my cloak!'

'This cloak,' said Bouda, 'brought by a Roman boy from Rome full of Roman gemstones is what paid for the good bread and beer you have been enjoying over the past few days.'

Bouda let the cloak slip to the floor of the chariot. 'And finally,' she turned and gestured towards a figure in a white hooded cloak striding out from the woods. 'The gods have sent us a new and younger Archdruid! This is Raven,' she said, 'son and successor of Snakebeard. He has come up with a better philosophy, a better way of life. Let him tell you!'

A cheer greeted Castor as he stepped up onto the chariot next to Bouda's, the one with the white ponies.

Fronto touched the statue of Jupiter and prayed, 'Please may they believe he is a Briton and a Druid.'

'You have come,' said Castor in Brittonic, 'full of fire and courage.'

'And beer!' quipped a muscular warrior near the front.

Castor nodded. 'And it would be wrong to send you home without release. Therefore let us begin games, to see which tribe is best. Instead of throwing spears and arrows to pierce, let us fire them at trees to see who is best.'

The warriors looked at each other uncertainly.

'Instead of driving our chariots at Romans,' said Castor, 'let us race against each other as they do at the Olympics. Instead of kicking the severed heads of our enemies, let us kick a ball. But let us do it,' he added, 'on the other side of this hill where there is a level meadow beyond the trees.' He gestured to the south on his right. 'Let us go there now. Let us make games, not war!' Castor said it again. From her chariot, Bouda cried, 'Make games, not war!' like a chant.

Instantly, the Britons took up her cry with enthusiasm.

MAKE GAMES, NOT WAR! They chanted, and some of them were already heading into the woods towards the south.

In the cheerful confusion Fronto did not hear the warning shout. But something made him look round.

And what he saw made his heart turn to wax.

Somehow, Snakebeard had escaped. His white robes were spattered with blood and he held a golden sickle in his hand. He was charging towards Bouda and Castor and screaming for revenge.

Chapter Forty-Three
ESSEDUM

Fronto watched in horror as the Druid chief leapt up onto Bouda's chariot. His blue snake-beards swung beneath a face contorted with rage. 'If I can't have the governor, you will do!' he cried. 'Drive!'

'No!' cried Castor. He jumped down from the back of his chariot and stepped up onto hers, trying to pull Snakebeard away. Bouda gasped as Snakebeard struck Castor's head with the handle of his sickle. Stunned, the youth slumped to the webbed leather floor of the war chariot. Bouda's scream was cut short as Snakebeard hooked his left arm around her neck .

'Drive!' Snakebeard thrust the reins into her hands and kicked the brake free. Alarmed, the ponies moved forward.

One of the Druid youths ran in front of the chariot to stop it, but was knocked aside by the right-hand pony. The team must have sensed an untrained hand on the reins, for within moments they were galloping full pelt down the hill. Now the warriors were yelling and running to get out of the way.

Bouda screamed again, and this time Fronto was spurred into action. He ran downhill after the chariot.

He had to dodge warriors and once he jumped over a blue-and-red-painted youth who had been knocked down. He was getting closer, for the ponies were still forging a path through the warriors.

'Stop him!' Fronto shouted at the Britons. 'He'll hurt Bouda!'

But without clear commands, the warriors were confused and stared at him stupidly. Three men with reddish-brown hair and black-and-white painted faces stood in his way and he had to run round them.

Then he heard a sound that stopped him in his tracks: the sound of marching feet on the fine Roman road. The governor was coming! Fronto scanned the cloudy sky, but saw no warning arrow. He looked back at the woods, but saw no figure high in the trees. Something must have happened to Vindex and his fire-arrows.

Fronto knew if the Roman soldiers saw Britons dressed for battle, they would certainly attack. He cupped his hands around his mouth and yelled, 'Get out of sight! The Romans are coming!'

Turning back, he saw that Snakebeard's chariot had found a place to cross over the ditch and was heading south along the Roman road.

Fronto's shoulders slumped. He would never catch them on foot.

Now he could hear the marching song.

Glancing left – to the north – Fronto saw a banner rising up and then the first of the soldiers crested a hill after it. It had started to rain and they were chanting something about Britannia and its weather.

Fronto hid behind a poplar, then turned and looked behind him, back up through shrubs at the sloping hillside. A moment before it had been covered with war-painted Britons. Now it was empty and still. Even the man crushed by the chariot was nowhere to be seen.

But there were some figures up by the backdrop of trees, where the grassy slope met the woods. They were standing and kneeling around a body.

Vindex! Was it Vindex? Fronto left his hiding place behind the poplar and ran back up the grassy slope past the charred remains of campfires and the marks of tent pegs.

It was now raining, but Fronto barely noticed. As he came closer he uttered a prayer of thanks: Vindex was alive! He was kneeling beside a body, his blond head bent in grief.

But whose body was it?

Chapter Forty-Four
BELTANE

'Cicatrix!' cried Fronto.

He had reached the top of the slope and could see the centurion's ugly head in Vindex's lap.

'Is he dead?' Fronto fell to his knees on the grass.

'Not quite.' Cicatrix gave a weak, gap-toothed grin. 'But I'm done for. That bloody Druid had a trick up his sleeve. Literally. Cut through his ropes with a sickle on a cord around his wrist. Old barbarian trick. Should have checked.'

'You can't die!' cried Fronto. 'You have to teach me to be brave.'

'You have your own courage, son,' said the centurion. 'Just remember: Fear is the scout, Honour is your commander . . . You, too, Vindex,' said the dying centurion. 'Make me proud . . .' His face was a ghastly white and his voice very faint. Raindrops splashed onto his face and Fronto heard him mutter, 'Bloody British weather . . .' Then he gave a kind of rattling sigh.

'He's gone,' said Vindex, looking up.

For the first time, Fronto noticed that his friend's face was almost as white as Cicatrix's. There was a bloody rag wrapped around his left forearm.

Dancing Wren stood behind him, tugging her curly hair in grief. 'Your friend Vindex was very brave,' she told Fronto. 'He came down from the tree to try to help.'

'I saw it happening,' gasped Vindex. 'But I couldn't use my arrows. Too many branches in the way.'

'Sneezing Vole is hurt, too,' said Nimble Tree. 'He twisted his ankle trying to stop the chariot. We want to take them back to Mistletoe Oak where we can put healing leaves on their wounds.'

'Yes,' said Fronto. 'Please help them. Take the horses!'

'No,' said Vindex. 'You take the horses. You have to save Bouda.' Even in pain his eyes were still smiling.

'There's the other chariot.' Ursula pointed.

'We don't even know where Snakebeard is taking them!' cried Juba.

'He must be going back to the Sacred Grove,' said One Ember. His face was very pale. 'Where we built the wicker man. Tonight is Beltane, when we purify with fire.'

Fronto felt his blood sink. 'You mean . . .?'

'Yes,' whispered Nimble Tree. 'We think he's going to burn your friends instead of the governor.'

They all looked at each other in horror.

'No,' said Ursula suddenly with such conviction that they all looked at her in surprise.

Her face was lifted towards the grey sky and her eyes closed. 'Last night in Bouda's tent,' she said, 'I had a dream. I saw a forest with skulls on the trees. I think that's where he's going.'

'There is a place called Skull Forest,' said Sneezing Vole. 'Full of very dark magic. It's half a day to the west, near Corinium.'

Ursula opened her eyes. 'That's where he's going,' she said firmly. 'I'm sure of it.'

'How do you know?' asked Juba.

She looked at them solemnly with her grey-green eyes. 'I just know.'

'I think he's going back to the grove near Mistletoe Oak,' said One Ember. 'It's much closer.' He swallowed hard. 'That must be why he told us to make the trunk of the man hollow.'

'That must be where he's headed,' said Juba. 'It's the right direction and it's much closer. Let's go there.'

Fronto clenched his fists. 'No!' he cried.

Juba and the others looked at him.

'What if Ursula's right?' said Fronto. He looked at Ursula. 'Are you sure?'

She shook her head. 'All I know is what I saw in my dream.'

'We can't take any chances,' said Fronto. 'Juba, you go to Mistletoe Oak and the Sacred Grove. But I'll go to Skull Forest, just in case.' He looked at the young Druids. 'How do I get there?'

'Take the road north,' said Vole. 'Perhaps ten miles out there is a rank of six tall elm trees on the left hand side of the road. Raven took me there once to show me why he feared Snakebeard.'

'Then Raven knew Snakebeard wasn't really his father?' Juba said.

'No, but he was beginning to question Snakebeard's view of the world.'

'How do you get to Skull Forest?' said Ursula.

'When you get to the six elm trees, go down a track between the middle two trees and across a sulphur stream.'

'I can drive a chariot, and I know I can find it,' said Ursula. 'I'll drive you.'

'All right,' said Fronto. He felt sick at the thought of confronting Snakebeard in a place called Skull Forest. But the thought of dishonour made him feel sicker.

'I'll go with you, too,' said Vole.

'You're hurt,' said Dancing Wren. 'You can't.'

'It's not too bad.' Vole stood up, then gasped and had to steady himself against a tree.

'No,' said Fronto. 'Ursula and I will go. We'll be faster with less weight.'

'Take your armour,' said Vindex. 'And your bow and arrows. They're in the horse's pack.'

'Good idea,' said Fronto and turned to the young Druids. 'Take care of these two,' he said indicating Vindex and Vole. 'And take his body?' He looked down at Cicatrix. 'He's been paying into a burial club for twenty years and is due a proper burial with a tombstone.'

Ursula held out her kitten. 'Can someone take Meer? And look after Loquax? I left him in his cage, back in the roundhouse.'

'I'll look after Meer,' said Dancing Wren. 'And I'll make sure no harm comes to Loquax, either.' She took Meer into her arms while the other young Druids started to help Vindex and Vole towards the horses.

Fronto turned to Ursula. 'Are you sure you can drive a chariot?'

Ursula nodded.

'Make sure the ponies are ready, then,' he told her. 'I'm just going to get my new armour.'

Chapter Forty-Five
SIMULACRUM

Fronto and Ursula reached their destination at dusk, when the exhausted ponies stopped of their own will. Fronto pointed. 'That's why they call it Skull Forest.'

The forest stood like a black wall of prickly holly, ancient elm and poisonous yew. Nailed to the trunks of the tallest elm trees were the sightless and grinning skulls of men. Some had scraps of skin and hair attached.

'Ugh! It's horrible!' Ursula turned her head away. A moment later she pointed. 'Look! There's the other chariot. And the unyoked ponies . . .'

Fronto looked at his little sister in wonder. 'Your dream was right,' he breathed. 'Like a prophesy.' Then his stomach writhed as he realised what this meant. 'Snakebeard is here. He must have gone into the forest on foot. And we must, too.'

He stepped down from the chariot, and told himself that his knees were wobbling because they had been riding for three hours straight.

'Help me put on my armour?' he asked Ursula.

It was strange having his little sister help him put on the heavy tunic of bronze scales. Its weight reassured him, and when he put the helmet on, he felt like a soldier again.

He knew they had no time to lose, for the sky was growing dark. He took a deep breath, uttered a prayer and looked for the best way into Skull Forest.

He chose two lofty elms without skulls attached and used them as his entry, tapping right, left, right.

It was dark in Skull Forest, almost as dark as night.

Above him, thick branches formed a roof. With his padded helmet he could hear only the sound of his own breathing but his nose caught a whiff of mouldy leaves and burnt branches. Skull Forest made the Deathwoods seem like a sunny glade. There was something more than damp, decay and darkness here. Something more than death. For the first time in his life he felt Evil as a presence.

Something touched his arm and he whirled, an arrow automatically notched and ready.

It was only Ursula, her eyes very wide in the gloom. 'Do you hear that?'

He replaced the arrow and took off his heavy helmet.

Now he could hear the faint beat of a single drum.

They followed its sound through the tangle of briars and dark trunks and presently Fronto could see the flickering yellow glow of a fire. The drumbeats were coming faster, like the heartbeat of a man who has moved from a walk to a run. The chanting seemed more urgent, too.

Now he could see a bonfire burning in the heart of a crudely circular clearing. Behind it towered a wicker man, twice as tall as the one the villagers had burned at Samhain half a year before. In one arm it held a stick meant to be a thunderbolt. It was Taranis!

Fronto put up his hand and then turned with his finger to his lips. Ursula nodded, wide-eyed. Her eyes gleamed in the firelight and he realised how dark it had become. He turned back to look at the scene in the clearing.

A single figure moved around the fire, chanting and beating a small drum held against his waist by the crook of his left elbow.

It was Snakebeard with his three blue beard braids and his hair in stiff spikes and his blood-spattered white robes.

'Where are Castor and Bouda?' Fronto whispered. 'I don't see them.'

'There!' gasped Ursula. 'They're in the wicker man.'

Fronto squinted and his blood grew cold. He thought he could see their faces peering out from the wattle torso of the woven man.

Unlike Soft Hill's leafy wicker man, this one was smooth and sculpted, almost a work of art. But it was also a deadly trap. He knew that once a torch was put to it, there was no hope of escape for those trapped inside.

Fronto shuddered. Of all the ways to die, burning alive must be the worst.

He tried to remember the advice Cicatrix had given him but all he came up with was an echo in his head: *You can do this.*

'I can do this,' he told himself. 'I can do this.'

Now Snakebeard was beating the drum as fast as the heart of a sprinting man. Fronto's heart matched its pace until, abruptly, Snakebeard stopped beating. He put down the drum and picked up a long staff. It was wound with ivy and at its end was a gummy mass of black tree sap. The moment the Druid put this end into the fire, the flames took hold.

'We're too late!' cried Ursula. 'We'll never get to them in time.'

'The gods haven't brought us this far for nothing,' said Fronto. 'I'll deal with Snakebeard. You circle around and try to set them free. Use the trees and darkness as cover. Here!' He pulled a dagger from its sheath on his left hip. 'Take this. But be careful . . . it's sharp!'

Fronto watched Ursula melt into the black forest.

Then he pulled an arrow from his belt quiver and notched it.

Snakebeard had been lifting the flaming torch to the heavens in prayer. Now he turned towards the wicker man. Castor and Bouda were peering through the branches of their woven cage, looking down at the Druid.

'With your help, Apollo,' Fronto prayed, 'I can do it.' He fixed his gaze on the white figure of the Druid. Then, carefully calculating distance, wind and trajectory, he loosed the arrow.

The arrow flew harmlessly into the dark woods beyond Snakebeard.

The Druid had not even noticed. He continued to stride towards the wicker man, flaming torch in hand.

Then Bouda began to scream.

Chapter Forty-Six
MALEDICTA

When Fronto heard Bouda scream, he stepped out of the black woods and shouted, 'How could you burn the girl you were going to make a queen? And your own son?'

Snakebeard stopped and turned his black gaze upon Fronto.

It was the terrifying face from the Deathwoods.

It was the face of the male gorgon from the sanctuary at Aquae Sulis.

It was the face of Medusa, and it made him freeze in terror.

'She's not of Boudica's blood and he is not of mine!' sneered Snakebeard. 'I was going to make them great, but they betrayed me. So I cursed them. And now I will curse you!'

With a trembling hand, Fronto drew a second arrow from his belt quiver.

'In the name of Taranis,' screamed Snakebeard, pointing at him. 'May your hands wither and your bones become water. May you never sleep again but writhe upon a bed of torment. May rats eat your flesh from without and worms eat your flesh from within while you still live.'

Fronto stood frozen by the horror of the curses.

Then Snakebeard made his mistake. 'I curse your brother and sister, too,' he spat.

'No!' shouted Fronto. He drew back the bow and released the arrow by instinct.

He did not wait to see if it hit its mark; he knew it had. He charged across the clearing towards the unholy cage and the sound of Bouda screaming.

And now Snakebeard was screaming, too. An arrow in his shoulder had spun him round and the flames from his torch had caught the hem of his robes. He was trying to beat out the fire but only succeeded in spreading the flames to his loose sleeves.

For a moment he was flapping his fiery arms like a bird, screaming and cursing as he tried to escape the agony of the flames. When he realised it was hopeless he turned and staggered towards the wicker man, his burning arms outstretched, intent on reaching it before he died.

'Fronto! Help me!' came Ursula's voice from behind the wicker man. 'I can't open it.'

'Fronto!' screamed Bouda. 'Quickly!'

Groping among the arrows at his right hip, Fronto felt the thicker shaft of a horse arrow. This was the one with a terrible U-shaped blade that could stop a charging cavalry horse in its tracks.

He fired it at Snakebeard and the man finally went down, his flaming right hand only inches from the wicker cage.

Fronto sprinted across the clearing and joined Ursula at the back of the wicker man. She was sawing at the rawhide fastening of a crude door in one of the legs.

'Fronto!' screamed Bouda from within the man. 'It's on fire!'

Running back to the front, he saw that flames were beginning to lick some dry hay that had been sprinkled at the feet of the effigy, presumably to help the damp wood catch fire.

'Ursula!' he cried. 'Give me your cloak!'

She looked at him for a split second, then nodded and tore it off. Fronto grabbed it and beat at the hungry flames.

'I've got it!' he heard Ursula cry. 'The door is open! Come out, Castor! Come out, Bouda!' she cried. 'Quickly!'

'We can't!' cried Bouda. 'Castor is still only half-conscious and our hands are tied behind us!'

'I'm going in!' cried Ursula, and to Fronto. 'You have to put it out or we'll all die!'

Fronto nodded grimly, still beating at small but hungry flames. He had almost extinguished them when Ursula's cloak caught fire. He tossed it away with an oath.

He had put out the burning hay on the right foot, but flames were still flickering by the unlucky left foot of the wicker figure. But now he had no way of putting them out.

Only his own armour-clad body.

Fronto offered a quick prayer to Jupiter.

Then he threw himself on the flaming hay at the foot of the wicker man.

Chapter Forty-Seven
PHALERAE

A week later, Fronto stood in the bright spring sunshine of the great amphitheatre at Isca Augusta.

He was wearing his best dress armour.

His fine brass lorica squamata had been badly scorched by the smothered flames, so Fronto wore a new tunic of iron chain mail, heavy but flexible. On his head was a conical helmet, polished to a mirror-bright shine. The bedraggled ostrich feather tail had been replaced with fluffy white ones. In the quiver on his right hip were twelve iron-tipped hunting arrows, three fire arrows and a horse arrow. He carried his composite bow in his left hand and rested his right on the pommel of his new sword: not a straight-edged legionary's gladius, but the leaf-shaped blade of an auxiliary. It hung just in front of the quiver on his belt.

On his left hip, near his dagger, was his tinder horn with its valuable cargo of glowing embers in ash.

'I've never seen so many people in one place,' murmured Vindex beside him. His new long-sleeved tunic hid his bandaged left arm, which was healing well.

Fronto nodded. The amphitheatre could hold six thousand and it was two-thirds full of people who had come to see the legions and the new recruits parading. Some were friends and family. Many had come from miles away.

Fronto, Vindex and the new recruits stood in formation at one end while different cohorts of the Second Augusta performed various marching drills, demonstrated a testudo and fought a mock battle with cork-tipped javelins and wooden swords.

Then it was their turn.

The new recruits marched and wheeled, showing how well they had learned Roman commands. Then came a display of skill by the Syrian archers. First the mounted archers fired arrows at targets from horseback. Then twelve of the best Syrian foot soldiers fired all the length of the arena, hitting every mark to great applause. Finally, Fronto closed the display by shooting a signal arrow into the air. He lit it with embers from his tinder-horn, waited for it to catch and then fired it high into the air. He judged the trajectory perfectly and the smoking arrow climbed up, flared red and then came thudding down a few feet from Quietus, who was wearing the side-to-side crest of a centurion and was announcing the display.

'AND NOW,' Quietus cried, 'NEW RECRUITS WILL BE GIVEN THEIR PERMANENT TAGS, TO SHOW THEY ARE FULLY ENLISTED.'

The horn's command brought the thirty-two new recruits into a neat line facing east.

The legate came forward, resplendent in white, gold and scarlet. He was followed by the senior tribune, the camp prefect and four civilians. Fronto was surprised to see two women among the party. As they came closer he saw one of them was his patroness, Flavia Gemina. She was walking behind a bald man in a toga.

'IT IS A MARK OF GREAT HONOUR,' blared Quietus, 'THAT THE GOVERNOR HIMSELF WILL GIVE THE TAGS AND PRIZES.'

As the bald governor started handing out tags further down the line, Fronto stood a little straighter. Only his eyes moved, wandering up to the tiered seats. He could see his sister Ursula wearing a new beaver-skin cloak and talking to Castor. Meer was on her shoulder and Loquax on her head. Fronto allowed himself a small smile that faded when he saw beautiful Bouda sitting beside his brother Juba. But she was looking at Fronto, not at Juba, and when she saw him looking her way she gave a little wave.

Then she pointed down and to her left.

Following the direction of Bouda's pointed finger, Fronto saw a lovely dark-skinned woman in a mustard-coloured stola, Flavia Gemina's freedwoman, Nubia. She sat beside a curly-haired man in a red tunic and eight children of differing ages and skin colours. Fronto recognised one of the children as Audax, Nubia's adventurous toddler. He wore a toy helmet and waved a wooden sword.

Fronto chuckled.

But his chuckle turned to a cough as the head centurion shot him a warning scowl. The governor had almost reached him and was just giving Vindex his tag. Now he turned to Fronto.

'Julius Mensa,' said the governor, reading the tag. 'I confirm your entry into the First Cohort of Hamians.'

In a low voice, the legate said, 'You probably didn't know that Cicatrix was in danger of being demoted. That's why he was given the lowly job of training recruits. But he fully redeemed his reputation in the end.' In a louder voice he said, 'Auxiliaries don't usually receive medals, but these phalerae have been awarded posthumously to Lucious Valerius Cicatrix and we would like you to honour him by wearing them this afternoon.' He hung a leather webbing with nine disks on Fronto's chest.

The governor and the others moved on, but as Flavia Gemina passed she stopped for a moment and squeezed the arm of a good-looking muscular man whose dark hair was salted with silver. 'Fronto, this is my husband, Jason,' she whispered. 'He's a close friend of the governor. You and your siblings and Bouda are to dine with us later in the praetorium, and tell us about all your adventures. You, too,' she said to Vindex.

Fronto gave a small nod. He kept his eyes straight ahead but he could see Vindex flushing with pleasure.

When the governor finished handing out tags and awards, Quietus made an announcement.

'FOR EXTRAORDINARY BRAVERY ON THE FIELD AND FOR SKILL WITH ARROWS, VINDEX AND MENSA ARE TO BE MADE IMMUNES WITH THE SYRIAN SCORPIONS.'

The crowd cheered and for the first time Fronto noticed the two beautiful Druid girls with older people, presumably their parents.

When silver-blonde Nimble Tree waved at him and curly-haired Dancing Wren blew him a kiss, his own cheeks grew hot.

Suddenly the crowd gasped as a dark brown bird with white patches on his wings flew down and landed on the top of his helmet. '*Carpe diem!*' cried Loquax. '*Carpe diem!*'

Everyone laughed and Fronto grinned. He glanced back up at Ursula and noticed Bouda gaping at the Druid girls. When she saw him looking, she grinned and blew a kiss, too.

Fronto's cheeks grew even hotter. Soon he would have to pray for another type of courage.

WHAT THE LATIN CHAPTER HEADERS MEAN

1. **DRUIDES** – druids
    A mysterious class of priests active in Britain and Europe a few centuries before and after Christ, they left very little record and no writings

2. **LARVA** – ghost
    Romans believed that ghosts haunted certain places; the word also means 'mask'

3. **VICUS** – village
    When Romans arrived in Britannia, they found most people lived in small villages of thatched round houses with animal pens and fields nearby

4. **FOCUS** – hearth fire
    Most roundhouses had a hearth fire at the centre, for warmth, cooking, light and comfort

5. **GEMMAE** – jewels
    Romans loved gems and jewels; they have been found in drains, bath-houses, graves and many other places in the Empire

6. **AQUAE SULIS** – Bath Spa
    The site of a hot mineral spring with a temple sacred to the joint British-Roman goddess Sulis Minerva

7. LORICA SQUAMATA – fish-scale armour
    *This striking form of body armour, was made by sewing
    metal scales on leather*

8. APODYTERIUM – changing room
    *Romans loved their public baths and every bath-house had
    a changing room where you could leave your clothes and
    shoes, at the risk of them being stolen*

9. FONS SACER – sacred fountain
    *You can still visit the sacred fountain at Bath Spa which
    pours out hundreds of gallons of steaming hot water every
    day; you can't bathe in it, but you can drink it*

10. FRICATIO – massage
    *A session at a bath-house could take many different forms
    including a steam-room, cold plunge and swimming pool
    sometimes finished off with a rubbing of the muscles*

11. AUXILIA – allied troops
    *Troops composed of non-Roman allies often served
    alongside Roman legionaries; auxilia means 'helpers'*

12. INCENDIUM – bonfire
    *Since the Stone Age, large controlled fires have had deep
    significance in marking changes of season for farmers,
    shepherds and cattle drovers*

13. SAMHAIN – ancient autumn festival
    *A Gaelic word pronounced 'SAH-win', this late autumn
    festival ushered in winter and may have occurred before a
    Day of the Dead, like our Halloween*

14. FLUMEN SABRINA – Severn Estuary
The Latin name for the body of water that divides England and Wales

15. ISCA AUGUSTA – Caerleon
Also known as Isca Silurum, the fortress at Caerleon was one of the three big legionary bases in Britannia in the late first century after Christ

16. OPTIO – junior officer
The optio was the centurion's 'chosen' right-hand man and carried a long straight staff with a round knob at the top

17. CENTURIO – mid-level officer
The centurion was in charge of a 'century' of men and carried a short, twisted vine-stick staff

18. SIGNACULUM – little identifier
New recruits to the Roman army were given a temporary 'dog-tag' of lead inscribed with their name and details

19. NOMINA – surnames
Romans sometimes adopted new names instead of their given names, though both would be recorded

20. SAGITTARII – archers
No hard evidence has yet been found, but auxiliary troops of Syrian archers may have arrived in Britannia by the late first century

21. BARDUS – singing storyteller
In a culture where most people did not read, the bard would have been a record-keeper, newscaster and teacher as well as an entertainer

22. NARCISSI – daffodils
One of the first flowers of spring, the narcissus was named after the mythical boy so beautiful he fell in love with his own reflection

23. PAX ROMANA – Roman Peace
Established by the Emperor Augustus a little before the birth of Christ, this was a policy of using armed forces to keep peace in the Roman Empire

24. VIOLARIA – banks of violets
Romans loved to adorn gods, goddesses, victors and friends with wreaths of flowers and leaves, all of which had different meanings

25. CORNICEN – horn blower
In the Roman army, horn calls were used for all sorts of signals, including reveille (wake up)

26. VITIS – vine staff
The centurion carried a heavy, twisty vine staff and did not hesitate to use it if someone under his command needed to be disciplined

27. TESSERA – password
The word can mean 'piece of mosaic' or 'dice', but in an army context it meant the small board on which a password was written

28. DEFECTIO – desertion
   Desertion was harshly punished in the Roman army;
   according to regulations the deserter's own bunkmates had
   to kick him to death

29. SOCII – followers
   The word 'socius' can also mean ally, comrade or friend,
   most often in a military sense

30. TINTINNABULA – bells
   Wind chimes with bells were considered good luck because
   the sound was apotropaic, i.e. it 'turned away evil'

31. VISCUM ALBUM – mistletoe
   According to Julius Caesar, Druid priests would use a
   golden sickle on the sixth day of the moon (i.e. a half
   moon) to collect this parasitic plant for use in potions

32. QUERCUS – oak
   Pliny the Elder tells us that the Druids held nothing to be
   more sacred than mistletoe growing on an oak tree

33. POTIO – potion
   Kids, do NOT try to make a potion like the one Ursula
   drinks: mistletoe and mushrooms can be poisonous!

34. TRIBUS – tribes
   Natives of Britannia in the first century did not think of
   themselves as British but rather as members of specific local
   peoples, e.g. Belgae or Iceni

35. FASCINATIO – enchantment
The closest concept to 'brainwashing' in Roman times was probably the idea of being enchanted by a spell, curse or potion, or combination of these

36. BELLATORES – warriors
Warriors in Britain mostly went barefoot and half-naked with only light wicker shields, hunting spears, swords and daggers.

37. APOLOGIA – defence
The word comes from Greek and does not mean an apology in the sense we know it but an account of why the speaker believes and acts a certain way

38. GEMINI – twins
Castor and Pollux were twins from Greek mythology; their father was Zeus and their mother was Leda

39. CONSILIUM – plan
The word can also mean a 'debate' or 'decision'; we get our word 'counsel' from it

40. LUNA – moon
The original Roman calendar may have been lunar, so that the first day of a month was always the day of a new moon and the Ides fell on a full moon.

41. BOUDICA – famous warrior queen
We know about the famous Iceni warrior queen from only a few brief sources, but it seems that same other tribes in Britannia had female leaders

42. GENII CUCULLATI – hooded spirits
A mysterious trio of hooded figures found on sculpture and altars in Britannia and elsewhere in the northern Roman provinces

43. ESSEDUM – chariot
Remains found in graves of rich Britons show that chariots would have been light and flexible, made of ash, oak and rawhide with bronze and iron fittings

44. BELTANE – ancient spring festival
Another Gaelic word, this festival celebrating the beginning of summer often involved various forms of fire for purification and protection

45. SIMULACRUM – effigy
Julius Caesar and Strabo write of men being put inside giant wicker men and then burned alive as sacrifices

46. MALEDICTA – curses
Spoken curses were believed to have enormous power in ancient Rome and Britannia

47. PHALERAE – medals
Sets of metal discs on a leather harness to be worn over chest armour were sometimes awarded to Roman soldiers as a mark of bravery or achievement